SHADOWS OF DESTINY

VEIL OF SHADOWS

BOOK NINE

M. R. PRITCHARD

About Shadows of Destiny

A journey of darkness and despair: Will Jed defy fate to save Shay, or succumb to his own ruin?

If looks could kill, Alastor would raze all of Hell in retribution. He didn't appreciate being sent home in a blast of light with everything he'd built destroyed, and he's going to do everything in his power to hunt down the half-breed who did it.

For Jed and Shay, Hell is filled with challenges, from hiding a stolen Angel baby to being a body double for the Queen; these two have their work cut out for them.

Now, if only Jed could get over his guilt for tearing Shay away from her normal life.

Jed and Shay must navigate a perilous path, where the line between savior and destroyer blurs, and the consequences of their choices echo through the infernal corridors.

Note to readers:

This book is a bridge between Veil of Shadows 5 & 6 and Jed and Shay's timeline. It brings both stories up to date and readies them for future books. This book contains chapters from Veil of Shadows: Nightjar. I couldn't write about Jed and Shay's time in Hell and skip over those scenes, they were too important in Jed and Shay's growth. Some have been expanded on and written more in depth for Jed and Shay's story. Enjoy, I'm happy you are here.

ONE

SHAY HAD READ enough books from her parent's library to know how to care for a baby. However, none of those books ever touched on the subject of caring for a baby Angel.

Jed was frantically drawing runes, casting protection charms, lining doorways with salt and ash. Sweat dripped down his face as he worked. He took off his shirt and wipe it away.

For the first time, Shay noticed the runes tattooed on Jed's skin glowed slightly as he worked.

The baby in her arms squirmed. Shay looked down at the dark haired child. Large blue eyes searched her face. Shay smiled. The baby simply stared as though it had seen something horrific.

There was blood on the blanket and small drops on

the baby's head. Shay licked her finger and wiped them off. She folded the bloody parts of the blanket away from the baby's face and checked him over for injuries. She lifted the folds of baby fat around his neck and arms but found nothing concerning.

The baby yawned and made quiet mewling sounds before his eyes fluttered closed and he fell asleep. Shay rocked the baby and watched Jed as he laid a line of salt across the balcony doors.

There was a thud outside the room. Something pounded on the door.

Jed crossed the room carefully so as not to disturb his hard work.

The pounding became louder.

"Who is it?" Jed asked.

"Let me in," a familiar voice replied.

"Not until you tell me who you are."

Shay's eyes were wide as she looked between the sleeping baby in her arms and the door.

Jed was right to be wary of the shit fest Meg had dropped into their arms. Memories of the battles with Angels and Demons flooded Shay. She couldn't imagine fighting like that with a baby to protect.

Two

Nero galloped across the wasteland of midwestern Hell. Inky seepage dripped down his flank and leg, leaving a hoofprint in the hard packed dirt.

He hadn't felt a thing through the tether to Shay in days. She was here and quiet. Nero had slowed his pace, the wound on his flank throbbing and aching. He surveyed the land ahead, searching for a cool pond to soak in. The ochre sun of Hell wasn't terribly warm, but it still exhausted the stallion. Nero didn't have a good feeling about the wound on his backside. The Crossroads Demon had clawed him back at the ranch and while the wound had festered slowly, it never felt as bad as it did now.

Nero thought about lying down to rest, but he was afraid he wouldn't get up again. Creatures he'd never seen before slithered in the shadowed forests of Hell. The dead walked here as well. The creatures kept their distance. He assumed it was because of the injury or the golden ring in his ear and around his neck. He was more than simply a stallion on the loose in Hell. He had rank. Something he never experienced on the Earthen plane. While Shay cared for him like he was her child, he still lived behind gates and fences. Freedom was new and while Nero enjoyed experimenting with his newly found free will, he missed the days at the ranch with Shay.

He'd slowed to a snail's pace without realizing it. Nero hung his head, afraid he'd never make it to Shay in time.

There was a sudden tugging along the tether that joined him to Shay. Nero's eyes went wide as he realized she was afraid. Whatever was going on, she still wasn't safe.

Nero dug deep down. He whinnied and shook his head, gathering strength he didn't think he had, then picked up his pace to a gallop again.

THREE

"It's Noah," the voice on the other side of the door sounded desperate.

"What do you want?" Jed asked, body tense and the short blade with runes gripped in his hand. He wasn't about to trust a soul.

"Did Meg bring you the baby?" Noah asked.

"Why?" Jed pressed his hand to the door and glanced back at Shay.

She shook her head, not wanting him to reveal anything. Not wanting him to open the door so they'd have to fight for their lives again. Shay's heart was beating faster than ever as she glanced around the room, looking for a way out or a plan.

"His name is Thrush," Noah says from the other side of the door. "He's my son."

Shay's gaze met Jed's.

"He's my son," Noah said again. "He used to have gray eyes like me. They're blue now. Sometimes that happens. Teari told us a baby's eye color can change."

Shay remembered that. She'd read about it in the medical survival books. A baby's eye color typically changed during the first year of life. The child resembled Noah in other ways.

Jed made a questioning motion.

Shay nodded.

Jed opened the door.

Noah stood in the hall. Blood and gore stained his clothing. He was disheveled, out of breath, and looked to be in despair. Noah didn't step into the room. He dropped to his knees in the hallway, buried his face in his hands and wept.

Neither Jed nor Shay knew what to do for him. After a few minutes, he wiped his face with his dirty shirt and stood again. He tried to walk into the suite, but an invisible force pushed him back.

"Let me in," Noah said, glaring at Jed.

"Maybe go get dressed and come back," Jed suggested. "He shouldn't see you like this."

"He's just a baby," Noah said.

"I know." Jed glanced at Shay as she rocked Thrush while he slept. "It's a memory that would stick, the day his father came to him distraught and filthy from battle, stinking of death."

"We'll wait here for you," Shay promised.

Noah disappeared, only to return in a few seconds, clean and refreshed. "Now will you let me in?" he asked.

Jed rubbed his boot across the line of salt at the door and motioned for Jed to enter.

"Fancy spells you've got here," Noah said, touching the runes marked on the doorframe.

"Don't," Jed warned. "We've been running for long enough. This predicament Meg put us in doesn't leave opportunity for the spells or wards to break. Especially with the baby here."

Noah pulled his hand away as though the doorframe were on fire. "You're right. What do you need?" Noah asked. "I'll do anything."

"We need supplies," Shay said. "A crib, bottles, formula, or milk."

"Nightingale was breastfeeding," Noah said.

"That could be problematic," Shay said. "Clothing, blankets."

"I can go find those things." Noah whispered, since he was leaning close to Thrush.

"Thanks," Shay said.

Jed continued warding the suite.

"I'll be back soon," Noah said.

————

"I found a crib at an empty house in Buffalo," Noah said as he passed supplies across the threshold to the suite. "I have to go back and get it."

"There are no stores down here?" Shay asked. "Nothing new?"

"There are some new things, but the crib looks like the one Nightingale had for him. It's some rich person's house. I doubt I'd be able to find anything like it elsewhere." Noah disappeared.

Jed set the bags that Noah had handed him on the kitchenette table.

"You want me to look through that stuff?" Shay asked.

Jed met Shay with a few steps and took the baby from her arms. "I'm not sure what any of that is."

Shay searched through the bags. Noah had brought them just about everything they needed. It all seemed new. Shay took out the bottles and washed them, then searched for the baby formula he'd brought back. There were three different ones. Shay released a heavy breath.

"You okay?" Jed asked.

"I hope so." Shay opened one box of baby formula and made a bottle. She found diapers, baby wipes, a clean outfit, and a fresh blanket. She brought everything to the bathroom before getting Thrush from Jed.

"What are you doing?" he asked.

"Bathing him." Shay laid Thrush on a towel on the bathroom countertop and began removing his bloodied clothing. "Help me check him over," she said to Jed. "We have to make sure he wasn't bitten."

Jed's gut pinched. He hadn't thought about the baby being bitten.

"Meg went to the Seven Kingdoms of Heaven, remember?" Shay asked Jed. "She went to help them with the fast dead." Shay removed Thrush's diaper, checking every finger and toe for injury.

Thrush woke, but he didn't cry. He simply stared at the two strangers.

Shay began talking gently to the baby. Telling him what they were doing. "You're going to get a bath and clean clothes. Then a bottle. How does that sound?"

"I don't think he can talk?" Jed said.

"That doesn't mean we don't talk to him. He learns to talk by his parents talking to him." Shay turned on the sink water and when it was warm, she plugged the drain and held Thrush sitting in the shallow water.

"I know nothing about babies," Jed confessed.

"I wouldn't expect you to," Shay said as she rubbed soap over Thrush's skin and rinsed him. "He doesn't look injured." She scrubbed his dark hair, wishing she had lavender baby shampoo like momma used to use at the ranch.

A knock on the door echoed.

"I'll get it." Jed left the room.

Shay could hear the familiar voice of Noah. There was grunting and the sound of moving furniture. A final thud in the bedroom sounded just as Shay was drying off, Thrush in a fluffy towel. She diapered and dressed him in the clean clothes Noah had brought, threw the clean baby blanket over her shoulder, and carried Thrush out of the bathroom to find an elaborate crib. It was round with a lace canopy and white linens.

"Isn't that a bit much?" Shay asked.

"Never," Noah said, walking closer and holding his arms out.

Thrush finally smiled as Shay passed him into his father's arms.

Noah whispered to Thrush as Shay went to get the bottle she'd left in the kitchenette.

Four

Alastor searched his hovel for the carving knife that Lucifer had gifted him. He'd hidden it long ago when Hell came under new rule. He knew the knife would draw attention being carved of basilisk bone with a blade of sharpened onyx. Lucifer had blessed the knife with darkness. Alastor was going to use it to kill the half-breed Angel who'd banished him from the Earthen plane with blinding light. The dumb ass probably thought he'd killed Alastor. He hadn't. Simply sent him home.

Alastor found the knife tucked behind the dresser. He set it on the bed and began packing. Urgency thrummed through his body. He'd wasted enough time gathering his strength once he'd become whole again. Luckily, he'd collected a stockpile of potions that would help him regain strength.

He found clean leathers, a bag that he filled with dried meat, and a skin of water. He secured the bone blade in the harness on his thigh and set out.

Alastor followed an old path that led him to the traveling roads of Hell. Long abandoned, he was sure he wouldn't run into another soul for a long time. The hovel in the mountains was secluded for good reason. He didn't want others seeing that he dealt in the skin trades. Plenty of times he'd brought humans to his hovel to sell. Lucifer didn't care. The meddling Deacons would though. Luckily, he'd stayed under the radar. With new rule came new scrutiny, especially after the Fast-Zombie War. The Deacons were out in droves, looking for lost souls. While Alastor hadn't brought a live human home since Meg took the throne, he also hadn't come across any Deacons searching his property.

He simply needed to get back to a portal and back to the Earthen plane. Then he was going to find that Angel-spawn and kill him. After killing and bathing in the creature's blood, he was going to steal that woman with the blowtorch blue hair. She'd look nice in his hovel, cooking at the fire or tied up near the door to his room like a living statue. Alastor licked his lips, thinking about the ways he could torment her, the ways he could use and punish her. It was too easy stealing her that night at the motel. She'd run into the snow covered parking lot like a deer in headlights. He wasn't sure what she was doing there, but something distracted her enough for an easy capture.

Alastor had plans for her and she'd ruined them all. She'd ruined everything. His contacts wanted skin, and he had none. It would take months for him to find more Demons to replace the ones that had died. It would take even longer to successfully possess men from the Earthen plane and twist them to follow his plan. Alastor was going to make Shay and the half-breed pay.

Walking through the mountain forest path was calming. Alastor missed the quiet days in the hovel before he'd gotten the taste of power. Once he'd drank from that cup, he couldn't go back. He didn't want to. He'd spent eons roaming the forest like a predator on the hunt.

Alastor noticed black sludge footprint ahead. He knelt and inspected the hooved prints, touched his finger to the inky fluid, and sniffed it. He closed his eyes. There was something familiar. Something he'd smelled before. Alastor sniffed again. Some Demons were gifted when it came to scent. Like Alastor. That was what drew him to Shay. She smelled like sugar and sunshine; pure, unlike so many human women he'd come across. He could smell the hint of her in the fluid on his finger. Alastor studied the tracks. Horse hooves. He sniffed the air. It was a Crossroads Demon. Either the Crossroads Demon was on horseback, or the horse was the Crossroads Demon. Either way, they smelled like Shay.

Alastor smiled at his good luck. He didn't need to find a portal because it appeared Shay was in Hell. He followed the tracks.

FIVE

THEN

LITTLE JED WAS EXCITED to have nearly a cup full of coins that he didn't notice the plainclothes Angel watching him. When a hand circled his wrist, Jed looked up into the stone carved face of an Angel man.

"No!" Clara shouted as she exited the restaurant.

Everything happened so fast. The Angel jerked Jed to his feet, spilling the coins across the sidewalk.

Jed knew he was supposed to yell and scream and fight, but it was broad daylight people on the street would help him. He looked up at the Angel, malevolence etched in his face. Jed took a deep breath and let out the loudest scream he could manage.

No one stopped to help him. The Angel began dragging him down the street.

Clara was shouting and running toward them.

Two police officers were ahead, watching from the opposite side of the road.

Jed screamed again, his little heart racing. He didn't know what to do. After everything his mother had taught him, when it came down to an emergency, he panicked.

Suddenly Clara caught up with them. She hit the Angel and shoved at him. "Let go of my son!"

"Hey," one of the police officers shouted. "What's going on there?"

"This man is kidnapping my son!" Clara shouted, grabbing Jed's opposite hand.

The Angel was squeezing Jed's wrist so hard that it hurt. He felt the bones of his thin arm flexing under the Angel's grip.

"Let go!" Clara tore at the Angel's hand as the officers approached.

An old lady intervened. "Leave that boy alone." She hit the Angel with her purse.

Jed watched grown men walk by or avoid them and move to the other side of the street. The men who could help, ignored them. Everyone except for the old lady with her shiny black purse as she swung it at the Angel, hitting him over and over again and cursing at him.

The Angel shoved the old woman and she fell. His grip loosened on Jed's wrist just enough for Jed to get his arm free.

The officers were lifting the old lady up. Then one approached the Angel.

"Oh God, baby, are you okay?" Clara knelt and rubbed her hands over Jed's cheeks. "Did he hurt you?"

Jed held up a bruised wrist, too afraid to talk.

"What do you think you're doing?" the officer asked the Angel, squinting. There was something about the Angel, he looked like any other man just taller and more handsome. But humans weren't used to seeing Angels and couldn't tell them apart.

"The boy was begging on the corner." The Angel pointed at Jed.

"It's not a crime," the officer said.

"It should be." The Angel stepped closer to Jed, reaching for him.

The old lady swung her purse and deflected the Angel's hand. "Don't touch that boy. You are something wrong. You don't belong here. You are evil!" the old lady shouted.

Jed looked at the graying woman's face then his mother's. Clara smiled and moved Jed away from the ruckus. She knew the Angel couldn't risk being found out. He wouldn't risk his secret. If this commotion kept up, he'd have to prove his identity.

Clara moved away little by little as the officers and old lady argued with the Angel. There was an alley just a few feet away. Jed watched a shopkeeper picking up the coins on the sidewalk that he'd dropped. His heart sank. That was hours' worth of smiling and begging, now they had nothing. He'd collected more coins in this town than ever before. Jed started crying softly. He rubbed the tears away as his mother took a few more steps closer to the alley.

The old lady smiled as she argued with the Angel and the officers. When the men started to look for Clara and Jed, she started swinging her purse again.

Clara stepped into the alley and pulled Jed with her. They disappeared, walking fast, and turning onto a side street. They went back to the small woman's hotel where they had rented a room.

"Good afternoon," Clara said to the woman at the desk with a smile like they hadn't just avoided tragedy in the street. She tugged Jed along until they reached their room.

Once inside, Clara locked the door and sagged against it. She sighed heavily before crouching and looking into Jed's eyes.

"It's going to be okay." She started unbuttoning his coat. "Let's look at that arm. Does it hurt?"

Jed nodded, fresh tears sliding down his cheeks.

"It's okay, baby." Clara pulled him in for a hug and kissed his messy hair. "We'll get cleaned up and get out of here." She pulled his arm out of the coat and inspected it. "You have a big bruise." She rotated his wrist and asked him to move his fingers one by one. "You know, before I was your momma I was a nurse. I worked with important doctors in a big city."

"Really?" Jed asked. He already thought the world of his mother after watching her save them all of these years. He never thought about her life before him. Children rarely did.

"Really." She kissed his bruised arm. "And this arm is going to be right as rain in just a few days. We'll just take it easy. Okay?"

Jed nodded.

"Let's get cleaned up and get out of here."

Clara began collecting the few items they had and packed them in the single suitcase she carried. She got a washcloth from the bathroom and washed Jed's face and combed his hair. "There we go, all fresh. Like nothing ever happened." She glanced at the clock. "We're going to miss dinner tonight. We'll get a big breakfast when we get off the train in the morning. Okay?"

Jed nodded, his stomach grumbling. He was always hungry and meals were sporadic. He knew they had to leave town after an Angel had found them. They'd probably spent too much time here already.

They'd boarded a train the usual way, by sneaking behind it and entering through the caboose just before it left. Clara charmed the ticket master into believing they'd packed the tickets.

If Jed hadn't dropped the cup of coins, they'd have enough for tickets tonight.

"Come here, son," Clara said softly, candlelight flickering in the small train car.

Jed yawned, tired from the day. He crawled toward his mother and lay his head in her lap.

"You were so brave today," Clara said as her fingers combed through his hair sending chills down his back.

Jed watched the candle flame dance. He didn't feel brave. He felt weak and sad. He'd been begging on the street for coins while his mother bartered at a restaurant for a hot meal. Jed was good at collecting coins. He was good at unlocking doors and starting engines. He was good at a few things. Except knowing when to run. He didn't want to leave his mother behind and his mistakes had cost them warm beds and hot meals before.

The train car jerked and the candle wax dripped to the side.

"Don't think about it, son," Clara said, scratching his head.

Jed couldn't stop thinking about it.

"Don't think about the coins." Clara combed through the other side of his hair with her fingers. "There's always more coins." She bent to kiss him on the forehead. "Always more coins but just one son of mine." Clara rocked him until he fell asleep.

It was that day Jed learned some humans were more of an Angel than the actual creature.

———

Now

THRUSH WOULDN'T TAKE the formula. After a few sucks on the bottle he gagged and puked. Then, after crying for hours, he fell asleep.

"Maybe he's teething?" Shay asked Noah.

"Nightingale never mentioned it." Noah's forehead creased in worry.

"Maybe something happened before Meg brought him to us?" Jed asked.

Noah shook his head. "I was there. He didn't get hurt."

"What about before you were there?" Shay asked.

"They were hiding in their bedroom." Noah paled

and swallowed hard. "Everything that happened, it happened while we were standing in the same room with them."

"Shhhh." Shay soothed Thrush as she rocked him.

"I'll go find something else to feed him," Noah offered.

"Good idea." Shay moved across the room and set Thrush in the elaborate crib. When she turned around again, Noah was gone.

Jed collapsed in a chair across the room. Shay fell onto the bed and threw an arm over her eyes.

Not five minutes had passed before someone started pounding on the door to the suite.

Shay sat up. "Make it stop. It's going to wake him."

Jed had a knife ready as he approached the door. He opened the door just a crack and found the Hellion named Skeele standing in the hallway. He was covered in blood and pacing.

"Meg needs help," Skeele growled.

"What kind of help?" Jed asked, gripping the knife.

"The life or death kind." Skeele was staring.

"Sounds like Meg." Jed lacked surprise. Meg was always in some deep shit that involved life or death. Hence why he and Shay were here now babysitting the Angel-baby she'd kidnapped.

"Are you coming?" Skeele shouted as he threw his arms wide.

Jed motioned for him to wait a moment and slammed the door.

"What?" Shay asked.

Unease filled Jed's gut. He'd never seen someone so worked up. "I think something bad has happened. I have to go."

"You can't." Shay's eyes were wide as she stood, reaching for him. "Don't leave us."

Shay knew how to survive the apocalypse of the Earthen plane, but Hell? Hell was a different matter–for both of them. She'd never been here before. Jed had never been here before. But he had to go now. Because if something happened to Meg, they were shit out of luck.

"Tell Noah as soon as he gets back," Jed said. "Noah will know what to do."

Shay nodded, blue hair falling over her eyes.

"I'll come back as soon as I can," Jed promised, stepping closer and gripping her arm. "I'll be back." He promised, wanting to kiss her. He didn't want to leave her here, alone. But he knew Noah would be back soon and the runes of protection around the suite were working. He wouldn't be gone long.

Shay nodded but worry glazed her eyes.

Jed backed out the door, checking the runes along the floor and around the door lock to make sure they were intact. He locked the door and turned to find the Hellion.

Skeele was pacing, cracking his knuckles, and looking thoroughly on edge.

"What happened?" Jed asked.

Skeele didn't answer; instead he grabbed Jed by the collar of his jacket and ran for the stairwell. Skeele ran down four steps at a time dragging Jed along. Jed tripped and stumbled, slamming his knee against the wall as he caught his footing.

"Let go of me, you asshat," Jed shouted, arms flailing as Skeele dragged him through the air on the descent. "You're going to break my fucking neck."

Skeele let go. "We need to move fast." He kept running down the stairs, the sound of heavy boots echoing off stone.

Jed followed, shaking off nerves. He didn't know what he was about to walk into. But if Meg was in the room, that usually meant he'd be walking into a shit show.

Skeele led Jed to a Hellion-marked door on the first floor. He pushed the door open and dragged Jed by the arm of his jacket, slower this time.

The metallic scent of blood was thick in the air. It only took seconds for Jed to see where it was coming from. There was a body on the bar, and it looked pretty lifeless.

"Come on," Skeele urged as he crossed the room.

As Jed approached the bar, a hand flew to his mouth. Shit. This was not good. Meg was dead. That meant he'd probably be dead soon as well. Coming here was a bad idea; they should have stayed on the Earthen plane. Jed cursed their decision. Shay would be in more danger with Meg dead and with the portals down, they'd never get back. Jed's mind was playing through a hundred gameplans.

"We need your help," Skeele said, rounding the bar.

Jed threw his hands in the air. "How can I help you with this?" Hands went to his hair and tugged.

"Do *something*," the dark Hellion in the room begged, his eyes wide and black. "She's going to die soon."

Skeele was pacing and growling and muttering in Hellspeak.

"I can't bring dead people back to life," Jed said, he didn't deal in death magic. "That's a different type of–"

Skeele crossed the room and ripped Jed's backpack off. "You know magic." He pointed at the tattooed runes on Jed's arms. "You know spells. You must know something that can help."

"Are you sure she's dead?" Jed asked.

Tukka checked her pulse again. "It's faint. Very faint." The large Hellion touched Meg's hair, leaving bloody fingerprints on her forehead.

The Hellions were savage creatures and as far as Jed knew, they didn't care about much. But it appeared they cared very much for this lifeless person. If only Meg knew.

Jed took his bag from Skeele's hands and poured it out on the portion of the bar that wasn't covered in blood. There were vials, papers, bags of sand, bags of bones, and other strange little trinkets. Jed found his spell book. He flipped through the pages, searching for something. Anything that could help.

"Come on!" Skeele pounded his fists on the bar. Empty glasses clanged together; the pings of glass threatening to shatter added to the angst in the room.

"I'm looking." Jed's fingers danced over the stained pages, his eyes scanned in rapid movements. "Ok. Ok. I think I found something that might help."

Jed went to work. He marked the wooden bar around Meg's body with charcoal, sprinkled sand, and arranged small bones near her head and feet. Last, he chose a small jar of white liquid that luminated faintly.

"What's that?" Skeele asked with a growl.

"Do you know?" Jed asked, one brow raised. "Some call it grace. Or at least, that's what I was told." He tilted the vial and the liquid inside luminated brighter.

"How'd you get that?" Skeele asked, eyes narrowed on the vial.

"I inherited it." Jed flipped the cap and stared at the two Hellions. There was a story behind the vial of Angel grace but he wasn't going to share it. "Now I need you both to shut up or join in."

Jed chanted ancient words from the book. He chanted words that sounded like ceramic crackling in a hot kiln, like ocean waves turned to ice, like the crack that declared the beginning of time.

The runes of sand glowed, the bones rattled like a rattlesnake tail. He tipped the vial onto his finger and pressed it to Meg's forehead. Chanting more, the words that originally sounded off and hard to wrap his tongue around became fluid and easier to annunciate the more he repeated them. The spec of grace on Meg's forehead pulsed. Jed was backlit in blue light as he motioned for Skeele and Tukka to join in.

The two Hellions made eye contact in apprehension but finally joined and repeated Jed's words.

Meg took a single breath. Her wounds oozed. Congealed blood dipped and formed circular crests. The spec of grace on her forehead glowed brighter.

Hope rose in Jed's chest. It was working. It was working!

Suddenly, Meg's wounds began gushing blood. Rivers flowed out of her. More blood than the Hellions had given her. Blood spilled onto the floor and the speck of grace turned from white to black. Meg's forehead smoked. Her body shuddered. The smell was putrid as the smoke billowed toward the ceiling.

"No," Skeele stopped chanting. "What did you do?"

He grabbed a rag from the counter behind him and wiped the dot of grace off her forehead.

"What the hell," Jed shouted. "You broke the spell."

"You were killing her," Skeele growled. "And now I'm going to kill you!"

Six

"She was already dead," Jed shouted. "I didn't kill her, you all did!" He pointed at Skeele and Tukka. Whatever trouble Meg had gotten into had nothing to do with him. Jed wasn't taking the fall for Meg's death.

Skeele ran around the bar, headed for Jed. "I didn't kill her," he growled. "I'd never kill her."

"Who killed what?" Noah's voice pierced the room. He appeared in front of Jed. Protectively. "You won't kill my man, Jeddio."

Jed's fast beating heart finally slowed. He hoped Noah could help fix this.

Skeele paused as best he could. It was hard to stop the killing motion of a Hellion, but he managed. Then he pointed to the bar. "Meg," was all Skeele said.

If a ghost could pale, Noah did. "No. No no no no no." He ran toward Meg. "What happened?"

"She just poofed into the room at my feet all stabbed up," Skeele said. "We tried blood. Jed used some bullshit spell that burned her face."

"She took a breath!" Jed thrust his hands toward Meg's body. "You saw it! We all saw it. The spell was working."

"It was not working," Skeele shouted back.

Noah held up his hands. "Just shut up. Both of you." He touched Meg's face, brushing off the burnt skin. If she was dead or in between, she might be in the Astral. Noah placed both palms on each side of Meg's head and closed his eyes. His image wavered as he searched the Astral plane for Meg. If she were there, it might mean they could get her back into her body.

Noah searched. He searched and searched and searched. He looked between every shadow of the void of the Astral but found nothing. The Astral was infinite, but there were places that he and Nightingale had created. Places that a wandering Meg might find familiar. He searched for them; a red tree by a stream, a kaleidoscope of stars above a hilltop, a hot tub at the top of a snowy mountain. Each place he visited tore at his gut. The memories of Nightingale were strong, and even stronger was the knowledge that he'd never get to spend time with her here again. Noah tried to push thoughts of Nightingale out of his mind. But memories are a spiral of emotion. It was a battle Noah barely won.

He felt a coldness surround him. A familiar coldness. Clea was nearby. Noah scanned the Astral shouting for Meg one last time. There was nothing. He had to go back. He had to go face Clea and tell her that Meg was nowhere to be found.

———

"OH CHILD," Clea's voice was full of sorrow. Her ruby red lips pinched together. Everyone stared at her. "It seems this curse is familial. We lose children too often here."

Clea knew about loss. Lucifer had lost Clea then Clea had lost Meg to the Earthen plane in an attempt to save her. Meg had lost her own child before it had ever been born. Clea and Meg's reunion was bound to be ended soon enough. It was all a vicious circle in this bloodline. Clea could see some of the future, with visions and omens; nothing she'd seen ever ended well.

"We have to do something," Noah said, moving his hands away from Meg's head. He didn't know what to say. At least Meg was here. At least they didn't have to search for her bones like Gabriel searched for twenty-five years for Clea's. Noah knew the story. At least they had a tiny bit of closure, seeing her here, like this.

"Have you tried everything to save her?" Clea asked, her image wavering, nearly transparent.

"We tried blood," Skeele said.

"I had a spell and some Angel grace," Jed began collecting his items and placing them in his backpack.

"Angel grace?" Noah asked.

Jed nodded. "It didn't work." He pinched the vial between his fingers and held it up to the light before placing it in his bag.

Angel grace might not have worked, but they had an actual Angel in the castle.

"I'll be right back," Noah said, just before he disappeared. "Don't touch her," his voice echoed throughout the Hellion lair.

Noah and Teari burst through the door of the lair. Teari ran to Meg's side. It didn't look good. It didn't look good at all. The air dripped with a metallic odor. There was so much blood and the remnants of a spell. Teari brushed the sand away and destroyed the runes surrounding Meg's body.

Jed shouted in protest, but no one paid attention to what he was saying. All of his hard work was simply brushed aside. He hated that he'd come here. Hated that these creatures had demanded him do something about the mess they'd created.

Skeele filled Teari in on what they'd tried. "Can you do something?" he asked.

Teari rested her arm on Meg's chest. "I can't do what I used to." She bit her lip, wishing she had hands. After all her years of healing, she had never felt so useless. She couldn't do a thing without her healing magic.

"Have you tried giving her fresh blood?" Teari asked.

Skeele's back went straight. Teari would have to be blind to miss his reaction.

"Did she fix Sparrow?" Teari asked. "His blood would be the best option. They have a bond."

"Sparrow is gone," Skeele said. "He's out of the picture."

Teari frowned. "Gone?"

Skeele motioned to the sky. "I'm assuming he went home."

"Crap." Teari stepped away from the bar and paced for a moment. She looked at everyone, studying them. Jed wouldn't do. Even with his mixed heritage, Tukka was unhinged at the moment. Her eyes paused on Skeele, the only one in the room who was semi-calm, but Teari could tell under his skin he was ready to lose it. The worry on his face was different, deeper than the worry of a bystander.

"What are you?" she asked, looking at Skeele. She

waved her nubbed arms in a flurry. "Who are you to her? There's a reason you're so upset that she's dying right now. There's something between you two?"

He cleared his throat and reset his demeanor. "Hellion First Command."

Teari knew the First Command was the closest to the leader of Hell. There was a bond. Duty and sacrifice demanded it. Even if Meg and Skeele never admitted it to each other. No matter how weak the bond might be, it would work the best. Without Sparrow, Meg was only tethered to Noah and being a spirit of the Astral, he didn't have blood.

"Your blood will do." Teari pointed at him with the nub of her right arm. "Give her your blood. Right now. Before she's gone forever."

It was a scene like Jed had never witnessed before as Skeele lifted Meg's lifeless body off the bar and walked out of the room.

Jed rubbed his neck, remembering Meg's bite.

SEVEN

SHAY PACED the room holding baby Thrush. Her arms rocked him quicker than she was comfortable with. Shay thought babies were fragile things that should be handled gently, but Thrush was only calm when he was rocked at a rapid pace. It worried Shay, that she might give him brain damage or that he might develop some strange fondness for being shaken when he got older. Shay tried not to think too deeply about it. The kid had barely survived being eaten during the Fast-Zombie war. Whatever methods she used to soothe him had to be better than what he experienced during that ordeal.

It had been weeks since they left the child in Shay and Jed's care. Every night they still checked his skin from head to toe for bite marks or wounds. They'd found none, of course. Only soft baby skin and the occasional diaper rash.

Shay paced near the door, waiting for Jed to return. She tiptoed around the markings on the floor, careful not to disturb the charcoal marks or piles of salt. Jed had protected them all for this long, she wasn't about to put them at risk.

Shay paused when she heard shouting from another area of the castle. She had a strong urge to leave the room and find Jed. She looked at the dark haired baby boy in her arms and remembered her promise. She couldn't leave the room, she could only hope that Jed would come back in one piece. He had to. He'd promised.

Shay glanced at the bottles drying near the sink. Thrush didn't want anything to do with the formula Noah brought. They'd tried everything. Every milk: cow, goat, sheep, almond, and coconut. Thrush didn't want any of it and what he did take, he puked up not long afterward. Shay's clothes were perpetually stained. Jed entered the splash zone, but he usually had towels ready to soak up the baby vomit. Thrush's cheeks were slowly shrinking in size, dark blue circles had started under his eyes. The kid wasn't necessarily sick, but from everything Shay had read, Thrush was borderline malnourished. If this kept on, he'd be completely malnourished quickly.

Noah was anxious about Thrush not eating. He spent most of his time finding something for his son to eat. They'd tried jars of baby food and infant cereals. Thrush would eat it, but it wasn't enough. He needed the milk for a few more months at least. He wasn't ready to switch to solid foods yet.

Shay saw shadows under the door. Someone was outside the suite. There was whispering, tapping, and then the door handle turned. Shay moved to the far side of the room, reaching for the spell cast shotgun with runes carved into the metal barrel.

The door opened.

Shay let out a sigh of relief as Jed stepped in and latched the door behind him. He leaned his back against the solid wood door and took a deep breath.

"Is she dead?" Shay asked.

Jed nodded.

"Shit." Thrush stirred in Shay's arms. She rocked the baby again. "What do we do?"

Jed made a face as he skirted the markings on the floor to get closer to Shay.

"She might come back to life. Skeele is going to try something."

"I don't think I want to know."

"It's probably better you don't. These people are freaks."

Shay tipped her head to her shoulder, a motion that told him they might not be so freaky. Shay had seen worse in humanity. Unfortunately.

Thrush started crying. Jed made a bottle of the most recent formula Noah had brought them. He passed it to Shay. Thrush pushed the nipple out of his mouth and gagged on the baby formula. Shay set the bottle down and shifted Thrush in her arms.

Tears started streaming down her face. "This kid is going to starve to death." Shay wiped at her face. "One day we are going to wake up and he's going to be lifeless in his crib. I just want him to eat something."

Shay was crying. Thrush was crying.

Jed stood nearby feeling utterly useless. He couldn't save Meg and he was sucking at keeping this kid alive. And while Shay was alive she was miserable in their current situation.

Thrush started nuzzling Shay's chest, leaving wet marks on her shirt.

"There's one thing we haven't tried," Jed said, reaching for his notebook of spells and magic. He flipped the pages.

Shay looked down at the baby and realized what he was talking about. "I don't think so."

"Why not?" Jed asked. "It's natural."

"I'm not his mother."

"You don't need to be his mother. Wet nurses rarely are."

"I've never done this before." Apprehension filled Shay.

"It can't be that hard." Jed paused on a page and tapped his finger on the paper. "I think I found something that will work."

"Don't you need my consent or something."

"This isn't permanent." Jed paused. "You don't want to try?"

Thrush whimpered in frustration, his little arms and legs were limp.

Shay couldn't watch him fade before their eyes. They'd both promised to look after this baby. "Just do it."

Jed's fingers danced in rhythmic spell casting; he chanted ancient words from his book.

Shay's chest started to feel warm and full. She looked down to see wet marks where her bra was.

"Okay, I think it's done," Jed said as he closed his notebook and knelt near Shay. "Do you want help?"

"Have you done this before?" Shay asked, tears dripping down her cheeks. This felt strange and weird and she wasn't prepared to hand over so much of herself.

"No. But that doesn't mean I'm of no help." Jed brushed his shaggy blonde hair away from his eyes. He set a hand on her knee.

Shay lifted her shirt and pushed her bra aside. She'd never breastfed a baby before, but she'd learned about it in her parents' survival books. There were plenty of chapters on delivering babies and placentas and keeping children alive.

Thrush latched on and ate, and for the first time in weeks he didn't cry or vomit. He simply ate until the tears on his cheeks dried to salt and he fell asleep making faint snoring sounds.

"Was it bad?" Jed asked, moving pillows behind Shay's back so she could get comfortable.

"It wasn't terrible." Shay scooted down in the bed until Thrush was lying flat and she could release him. She looked at Jed. "This is way more than what I signed up for."

"But look at all the fun we're having. I told you there would never be a dull moment with Meg involved." Jed crossed his arms on the bed and leaned forward from his sitting position on the floor. He and Shay were almost nose to nose.

"You should have warned me in Montana that if I followed you, I'd be stepping into some mega shit." Shay pursed her lips.

Jed smiled. "What better have you got to do? Kill zombies and pick dumpsters for food?"

"I didn't get my food from dumpsters. I grew it and hunted for it."

"Okay. But had you stayed, you would have never experienced this shit show. You'd be so bored."

"I wouldn't be lactating to feed an Angel ghost baby hybrid." She smoothed Thrush's hair away from his eyes and smiled, relieved that the baby had finally eaten something and kept it down.

"True." He reached out and touched her hair. "I did warn you though. I offered to bring you back. I warned you that hanging out with me was a very bad idea."

Shay sighed, tired from the long day and the tears. She didn't want to argue with Jed. She wanted nothing more than to sleep a few uninterrupted hours, but they needed to talk. "Tell me what happened downstairs."

Jed made a face, but he told her about trying to bring Meg's lifeless corpse back to life.

"What are we going to do?" Shay asked.

"We can get out of here." Jed was looking toward the window. "The front door opens. We aren't locked in here." He ran his hands through his hair in frustration. "Noah will do anything to keep Thrush safe. He has to help us. We just have to get back to the Earthen plane."

"You don't think it's safer here in Hell?" Shay asked.

"I don't know," Jed replied. "I thought it would be safer with Sparrow. But that plan has gone completely to shit."

"So we go back home." Shay tilted her head. "We find a way back home and take this baby with us?"

Jed stared at the sleeping baby in Shay's arms, memories flooding him. Memories of a lifetime on the run, a childhood on the run, his mother fighting to save him every day. That day she pushed him out of the moving train car, he lost her forever.

Jed rubbed his face in defeat. He couldn't force Shay into a life like that. He looked away, thinking. He could still wipe her memories and bring her back to the ranch. He didn't want to be a liar but he'd much rather protect her from the life Clara had. Shay didn't deserve that.

When he looked toward Shay again, she was sleeping. He touched the soft fabric of the bedsheets, remembering the moments of ecstasy being inside her. The soft noises she'd made, the way she felt in his hands. The way she made him feel strong and loved and desired.

Eight

Alastor stopped at a tavern that was pushed back into the forest. This was a place for Demonkind only, a place he'd frequented in the past. He was hungry and thirsty and wanted to get off his feet. He'd followed the horse tracks for the entire day. Judging from the distance between hoofprints, the horse had to be traveling at a decent gallop. Alastor would catch up eventually. The black substance was accumulating more and more with distance. The creature was bleeding and must have had some injury. Eventually it would slow, Alastor would bet on it.

Noise in the tavern ceased. Everyone set down their drinks.

"Did you feel that?" a deep voice asked.

"Something's happened," another voice said.

"She's dead. The Queen is dead." A Demon with four horns on the back of his skull stood.

"Fuck her." Another Demon with stubby legs shouted. "Now things can go back to the way it used to be."

A chair flew across the room and smashed across the back of the head of the Demon with the stubby legs.

In the corner of the tavern were three Hellion recruits, Alastor could tell from their clothing.

Something was happening. Alastor had felt the shift in energy. He looked out the window. The Veil between Hell and the Earthen plane was thinning again. If he needed to, he could find a hole and walk across. He drank his ale. He had a man and a woman to deal with. If the Veil stayed like this, it would make it easy for him to get back into business. No more sneaking across the portals in the night and bribing guards.

Alastor ate as the Demons in the tavern fought. Every so often, the tavern owner would throw a group of Demons outside to finish their fighting. Everyone had become considerably louder. The Hellion recruits took off, no doubt making their way back to the castle to check on their Queen. Alastor would have considered going to the castle to investigate but he had other things to do.

He paid his tab and left.

Alastor made his way back to the trail of horse prints that he'd been following.

There was another shift in the air.

Alastor looked around him. The Veil was solidifying again. The Queen did not die but something had happened.

He could see the Hellions flying and it took him a moment to realize that the hoof prints and the Hellions were going in the same direction.

If Queen Meg was keeping an Angel half-breed at the castle, something strange was going on.

With renewed energy, Alastor moved faster.

Nine

Meg flashed into the room.

"You're alive," Jed said with a full mouth as he chewed a bite of his turkey sandwich.

Shay stopped mid-bite and set her sandwich down.

Noah appeared next with inkpots and a handful of sterile needles. He dropped them in front of Jed.

"Let's go," Meg said to Jed. "Get your tattoo gun."

Jed turned to Shay, "I'll be right back."

"It's going to be a few hours," Noah warned, "at least. I'll stay with him."

Neither Jed nor Shay had left the room in days.

A lump formed in Shay's throat with the thought of being separated. She glanced at the door to the bedroom where Thrush was sleeping.

"It's fine," Meg said. "We just need some ink."

Jed crossed the room to grab his tools. "It's going to be fine," he breathed quietly to Shay.

Shay nodded and stood to check the wards and re-pour the line of salt across the threshold of the door.

Meg led Jed to the second floor.

There was an empty room near the stairwell with chairs and a table and good lighting. Meg opened the door and waited for Jed to enter.

It only took Jed a second to see Gabriel waiting in the corner.

"Oh no," Jed backpedaled toward the door. "Nope. Nope. Nope."

Meg grabbed his arm. Noah slammed the door.

Gabriel squinted at Jed. "Well, I'll be damned," he murmured.

"I have spent my life avoiding Archangels and you brought me to one." Jed was ready to lose it, his eyes wide with fear and anger. "Is this some sick joke?" He glared at Meg. "I knew I could never trust you, Meg. Never. The things I've done for you and now this?"

"Calm down, boy," Gabriel bellowed. "I'm not here for you." He frowned. "Damned surprised to see you upright and down in this realm," he raised his palms, "but the more days I live, the less this shit surprises me."

"He needs the runes," Meg said, holding out an arm. "He needs freedom from the other Archangels."

Jed tossed his equipment on the table. He glared at Meg. "This is not what I signed up for."

"We're in the same club," Meg moved closer to Jed. "Gabriel is my father. The other Archangel's are rallying against him, including Sparrow."

"Fucking Angels," Jed muttered, shaking his head. He pointed a finger at Meg. "You owe me big time for this." He set his equipment on the table and started prepping to tattoo Gabriel. "You owe me for the rest of your goddamned life."

"Done," Meg held out her hand, pinky extended. "Pinky promise. I am forever in your debt."

Jed jerked his hand forward, curling his pinky around Meg's and stared into her eyes. "I am a forbidden creature. They will always hunt me."

Meg nodded, understanding.

Jed picked up one of the inkpots that Noah brought. He set it aside and motioned for Gabriel to lay his left arm out on the table. "We'll do both," he said. "If you can handle it." Jed smirked.

Gabriel rested his arm on the table and Jed went to work with the buzzing of his machine.

"Would this prevent Sparrow from finding Thrush?" Noah asked.

"The runes?" Meg asked.

Noah nodded.

"I'd assume." Meg said. "But, wait. Are you suggesting tattooing a baby?"

Noah pressed his lips together and tipped his head in a maybe expression.

"I don't think that's a good idea," Meg said.

"Absofuckinglutly not," Jed said.

TEN

"MEG FOUND US A PLACE TO LIVE?" Shay asked Noah.

He kissed Thrush's cheek before replying, "Yeah. It's in a graveyard not far from here."

"A graveyard?" Jed stopped checking the wards and stared at Noah. "You want us to live in a graveyard."

Noah shrugged. "It's peaceful and safe. There's a chapel. It's like a cabin. I wouldn't let my son grow up in some awful hovel in the ground."

Jed and Shay glanced at each other.

"How safe?" Shay asked. "Meg has been on edge for a while now. I'll be happy to escape these four walls but I don't know anything about Hell."

"I'll stay close," Noah promised.

"And what about Meg?" Jed asked.

Noah nodded, understanding. "I'll tell her to stay away. She'll listen to me."

"Meg doesn't listen to anyone," Shay countered.

"I promise, she'll listen to me." Noah patted Thrush as he slept.

———

Shay stepped outside in to daylit Hellsky first. She looked up and took a deep breath. "I never thought it would feel so good to be outside again."

Jed touched the small of her back. "Even with this cold?"

Shay adjusted her backpack and rubbed her hands together before checking Thrush's snowsuit and hat to make sure the cold couldn't sneak in.

"Is Noah coming with us?" Shay asked.

"He's at the chapel, dealing with Meg." Jed began walking. He felt strange being allowed outside alone, but a shadow flying overhead reminded him they weren't completely alone. The Hellions were scanning from above.

"It's not too far of a walk is it?" Shay asked.

"Noah said maybe ten minutes." Jed shifted Thrush's weight as they turned down the empty road.

"Do you think we brought enough supplies?" Shay asked, making conversation. She'd spent hours in the kitchen collecting canned foods, fresh bread, and perishables. It seemed the kitchens of Hell weren't that different than the kitchens of the Earthen plane, just more rudimentary; no processed foods unless someone brought them back from their travels.

"If we need anything Noah will get it for us." Jed stepped over a large pothole. "Meg should get a road crew out here."

"She seems busy with a lot of shit," Shay said.

They walked, enjoying the icy chill of winter and the hollow noise their footsteps made. Jed and Shay had been locked up in their rooms for too long. The freedom was best enjoyed in silence.

"There it is," Shay pointed to a small building between the gravestones. "It doesn't look too bad."

"Like a chapel in a picture book," Jed said, his eyes landing on Meg in the distance. She was a few hundred yards away from the chapel, sitting with Noah. Noah's hand was on her shoulder. Meg looked utterly sad as she ate.

"You think he's telling her?" Shay asked.

"Yeah." Jed nodded. "She doesn't look very happy about being told she can't come near the baby."

"It must be hard for her after losing everything. Didn't you say she was from the Earthen plane?"

"She was. She didn't know what she was but the things she went through, no one should live through."

"Same for you." Shay touched Jed's elbow. "You've both had it pretty rough."

Jed smiled softly. "We've all had some trauma etched in our bones."

"So this is going to be our home forever?" Shay asked.

"For as long as Thrush needs us." Jed checked on Thrush who was facing outward in his arms. The boy had been quiet since they'd left the castle in the burning caves.

"He's fine," Shay said. "He hasn't had so many things to look at. Do you think he'll like living in a graveyard?"

"At least there's grass and trees," Jed said.

"There's fencing."

"To keep the dead from wandering too close." Jed's gaze went to the sky again. "The Hellions will be doing rounds to check the perimeter."

"Maybe we should get a guard dog or something," Shay suggested.

———

THE CHAPEL WAS COZY. Shay felt peaceful as she searched the rooms and acquainted herself with their new living quarters. There was a small kitchen, a bathroom, two bedrooms, a living room. She looked out the window to the expanse of grass out the back. There were no headstones obstructing the view, and for a moment Shay felt as though she were back on the ranch, washing dishes and gazing out the window as the Montana breeze blew the tall bluegrass into a swaying motion. Nostalgia tugged at her chest. She scraped her boot across the roughhewn wood floor as she moved to unpack her bag and put the food they'd brought away.

"Meg's gone home," Noah said as he appeared in the living room.

"Please don't do that," Jed said, holding the short hunting knife with runes carved into the handle. "I could have stabbed you." He gave an annoyed look before carving runes into the doorframe again.

"You don't need to deface the place," Noah said, watching Jed.

"If I trusted every person who attempted to give me a safe home, I wouldn't be here right now." Jed secured the knife in his belt and pulled out a Sharpie marker, marking the walls around the doorframe next.

Noah made a face that suggested perhaps Jed was correct in his statement. "Where's Thrush?"

Shay pointed toward the bedroom. "Sleeping. All that fresh air tired him out."

Noah moved toward the door.

"Don't you dare wake him up," Shay said, holding a glass jar of tomatoes. "That poor boy hasn't slept in weeks."

Noah stopped mid stride and turned. "Hey, he hasn't, so how is he sleeping now?"

"He just ate," Jed said, absentmindedly.

"Ate what?" Noah scratched his face. "Did he finally take the formula?"

"No." Shay set the jars in a cabinet. "Have you ever heard of a wet nurse?"

"Like from the movies back when women wore petticoats and bonnets and crap?" Noah asked.

"Yeah. Exactly that," Shay said. She turned, pointing to her chest. "Jed had a spell. And it worked."

Noah was staring at Shay's breasts stretching against her shirt.

"Hey." Jed grabbed a pillow out of the nearby chair and threw it across the room at Jed. "Don't stare at her boobs, you sick freak."

Noah scoffed. "I'm not the freak. She made me look. She pointed at them. What am I supposed to do? Ignore her?"

"Settle down, boys," Shay mocked as she continued unpacking her bag of food. "Are you going to be spending a lot of time here, Noah?" Shay asked. "Should we set up the other room for you?"

"Better not," Noah's shoulders dropped. "Meg needs me. I'll try to split my time with Nightingale gone. I'd like to spend as much time with Thrush as possible."

"Maybe stop working for Meg?" Jed suggested.

"I can't do that."

"Why won't she release you of your duties?" Shay asked.

"It's not that easy," Noah scrubbed at his hair. "Lucifer bound us. I'm tethered to her. Our souls are tethered. She calls, I show up."

"Always?" Shay asked.

"Every time." Noah sat on the couch and stretched his legs out.

"You could take Thrush to work with you," Jed suggested.

"With the type of crap Meg gets herself into? It's not for children. And if Nightingale knew, she'd kill me."

There was a long pause. Shay could sense something gloomy and brooding in Noah, similar to how she felt when her parents died.

"I'm sorry she died," Shay said. "I am, Noah. Life is hard enough."

"This is the afterlife for me." Noah looked at the ceiling.

"I guess the afterlife is hard enough." Shay put a container of milk in the fridge. "I never thought I'd ever say something like that."

Noah chuckled. "Me either."

Eleven

Life at the chapel was quaint and quiet. Jed and Shay brought Thrush outside for fresh air. The fencing obscured their views of the field behind the graveyard and the forest, but it was a minor discomfort. Thrush gained weight. He ate and slept and they'd fallen into a daily routine of breakfasts and lunches and long walks, Jed bringing Thrush with him to check the wards and runes around the house and property each day. Shay watched them from the kitchen window and thought how different and similar life was between Hell and the Montana ranch. She was glad she told Jed not to wipe her memories. She'd never get to experience these quiet moments. It was hard to think that she was in Hell after all.

Thrush was sleeping soundly in his crib as Jed switched off the nightstand light and collected Shay in his arms. He kissed her bare shoulder and his hands explored under her shirt.

"Again?" Shay whimpered when he touched her bare breast.

"It's been days." Jed leaned away and pulled Shay to face him in the darkness. "I like this. I don't ever want to lose it." He kissed her, slow and deep. "I want to touch you all day long but I can't. This is the only time we slow down."

The noise of footsteps interrupted them.

"Someone's here." Shay threw back the blankets. "Someone's in this room."

Jed rushed out of the bed as Shay turned on the light. A dark figure was leaning over the crib.

"No!" Shay shouted.

Jed ran toward the figure, blade in hand, lips ready to chant a spell.

Shay got a glimpse of the figure's face before it–*poof*–disappeared.

"That was Meg." Shay ran to the crib, tearing at the blankets as though Thrush might still be there. "Why would Meg take him?"

"The Nightjar stole Thrush," Meg said, her eyes wide and face pale. Her clothing was soaked and hair dripping wet.

"Tell me why I shouldn't trap you in the Astral for eternity," Noah was seething.

"You don't understa–" Meg tried to say.

"I told you to stay away from Thrush and you took him to another realm," Noah said.

"Why did you take him?" Shay asked.

"Yeah," Jed added. "Didn't you do enough damage already?" He'd watched Meg create more than enough problems.

"I had to get him baptized. He was going to turn into a Nightjar. I couldn't curse his entire life." Meg looked at Noah. "You knew. You knew what fate held for him without the baptism. I couldn't let him turn into something else. Something like Elise. Don't you want more than a jar of feathers to mourn? Don't you want more for your son?"

There was silence. Jed pulled Shay closer as Meg told them about the death of her unborn daughter. Sympathy flooded Jed. She could so easily have been his mother, Clara. That dead infant could have been him.

Twelve

Jed waited on the shoreline with Meg. Neither of them could fly like the others.

"This is ridiculous," Jed finally said. "Demore is playing with them." He watched Thrush hover over the water and Noah drift below him.

Jed crouched and emptied his bag onto the sand at the water's edge.

"What are you doing?" Meg asked.

"I have an idea." Jed laid out a red square of cloth. "I've been reading up on this. I think it's going to work."

"I'm not sure this is the time for experiments," Meg said.

"They're not experiments," Jed replied, annoyed. "They've kept me alive this long."

He arranged bones and small black feathers on the

square of cloth followed by vials of strange liquid, and finally, a stick of cinnamon that he lit with a flame and set to smudge.

"What will this do?" Meg asked.

Jed pointed to the water. "You said that's a conduit?"

"Yeah." Meg nodded.

"Then watch this." Jed chanted strange words. His fingers danced in rhythmic and repetitive motions. The water in front of them bubbled softly. Steam rose into the sky. A white, wispy form began taking shape.

"What is that?" Meg asked.

Jed chanted louder, stronger, and his fingers danced faster. He spat words that sounded like a hissing snake, that sounded like a baby's first cry; it sounded like the gasses of the sun churning.

The wispy form coming from the bubbles solidified.

It was Nightingale.

"Night!" Meg started to move toward her.

"Don't," Jed warned. "She's not here for you. I didn't call her for *you*."

Meg went still.

Jed had never met Nightingale but he was intrigued by the Angel Noah had fallen in love with. Nightingale wore a black crop top and tiny red gym shorts with white piping—straight out of the eighties. She had headphones resting on her neck and big, clunky roller skates. She turned, her dark hair flowing down her back. She glided across the pond, skating like she was at a disco. She twisted and turned so fast her image was a blur. She whistled a melodic trill.

Noah turned away from Thrush, recognizing Nightingale. Everything changed. There was electricity in the air. The light from the moon dampened to a dreamlike haze.

Nightingale glided toward Noah. She took him into the air as though there were an invisible elevator until Thrush floated between them. Thrush babbled as he recognized his mother. Nightingale whistled a gentle trill to Thrush before taking him into her arms and holding him close.

Plip-plop. Plip-plop. Plip-plop. Plip-plop. Demore came from over the treetops, fast. Her mournful melody getting louder and louder.

"Mine," she cried out. "My precious. My baby. My gift." The dark shadow of the Nightjar soared faster to meet Nightingale.

Nightingale held out a hand. She had a power that stopped Demore in her path. Nightingale's sweet, high-pitched chirping trills turned into guttural chatter.

"What are they doing?" Meg asked Jed.

"They're gonna fight," Jed said.

Nightingale pushed Thrush into Noah's arms and then she illuminated, drawing all of the light from the moonlight until she was a giant, glowing orb. Demore's shadows grew and blacken, her tendrils draping the canopy of the forest.

Meg was waving her hands at Noah, trying to get him to move back. Whatever the women were doing, they were getting bigger and bigger and drawing energy from around them.

Gabriel swooped down, white wings spread wide in all their glory, and grabbed Noah and Thrush, bringing them to the opposite side of the pond.

Lightning crackled between the twisting balls of energy that Nightingale and Demore had become. They rose in the sky; swirling, crackling, screaming, and crying. Their forms shifted and blurred. They twisted and jabbed. The wind picked up, blowing leaves and sticks into the air.

Meg stepped into the pond and dunked her head. There was something strange about needing the water to see Demore.

Nightingale sent a blast of light and electricity to Demore. The dark ball of energy shrank and shuddered in defeat.

The fight was over. Demore's cabin was dark, her shadowed form roiling behind the windows.

Nightingale dropped from Hellsky like a ballerina, landing elegantly on one foot. She glided across the water on her roller skates, twisting and turning. She stopped in front of Noah and bent to talk to Thrush.

Meg turned to Jed. "That was the best idea you've ever had," Meg began walking toward the shore. "You saved Thrush." She was smiling. Happy. Elated.

Jed smiled and shrugged a little. "Nothing can defeat a mother's need to protect her child."

"It was per–"

Meg never finished what she was trying to say. She was jerked backward and fell. She scrambled, grabbing at the shoreline sand and rooted plants.

Jed ran forward to try and help her but it all happened so fast. One moment she was there, the next she disappeared under the water.

"Where did she go?" Skeele shouted.

Jed pointed to the pond.

"She went under the water and never came out."

Gabriel frowned. "It's a portal. We went through it before."

"A portal to where?" Skeele asked.

"Babylon." Gabriel was moving closer.

"No." Skeele shouted as he dove into the murky pond water.

Jed's back went stiff. A portal straight to the Seven Kingdoms of Heaven and he was standing directly next to it. No. He would not partake in this.

Noah approached Jed. "Come on, man. Let's get you out of here. The Hellions will take care of Meg."

Jed nodded. He wasn't a coward but he knew his limitations. He'd worked too hard bringing Nightingale back from the ether. Tremors shook his arms. Jed felt ill. Sweat dried to his back giving him chills.

"You okay, man?" Noah asked.

"I need to rest." Jed stumbled as he bent to collect his belongings. "Need to get away from this portal." He couldn't defend himself in this state if an Angel came through for him. He didn't know if his aura would shine through after all the magic he'd used to bring back Nightingale. He was sure he was glowing like a torch.

Thirteen

Nightingale was thanking Jed and Shay for taking care of Thrush. She kept her face half-turned in an attempt to hide the scars from the Fast-Zombie War. They didn't seem to impact Thrush's recognition of his mother. He couldn't stop looking at her and babbling, clapping his little chubby hands and drooling.

Noah kept touching Nightingale like he couldn't believe she was real again.

The handle on the fence turned halfway before someone shouted "Ah! What the heck?"

Jed was closest to the gate and recognized the voice. "Meg?" he asked. "Is that you?"

"Yes it's me."

Jed opened the gate. "Oh, thank God. We thought you were gone."

Meg entered the fenced chapel yard for the first time since she'd been banished by Noah. "You were supposed to be at the castle," she said.

"They were safe with me," Nightingale said. Thrush had fallen asleep in her arms.

"Where's Teari?" Meg asked.

Noah nodded toward the door to the chapel.

Meg headed there, passing Shay who'd taken up conversation with Chel about survival gear and weapons. "Welcome back," Shay said.

Meg entered the chapel.

A few minutes passed when Teari screamed, "Meg! What are you doing?"

Jed and Shay made eye contact before running toward the door with Chel.

Teari was sitting on the couch with her arms crossed; the prosthetics had fallen.

"I knew we couldn't trust you in here. What did you do?" Jed asked.

"Oh, just performing a miracle," Meg said. "But I'm hurt, really. Why must you always assume the worst of me?"

Jed had plenty reason to assume the worst. But, he also jumped to conclusions quickly when it involved her. It was a side effect of living on the run and always anticipating the worst.

Teari held up her arms and everyone in the room watched as her hands regrew.

"I always assume you're up to something," Jed said. "But this is better than I was anticipating." He jabbed Meg in the shoulder as a playful apology.

"Oh my God," Teari exclaimed as she stood. "This is the best." She moved toward Meg and threw her arms around Meg's neck. "Thank you, Meg."

Meg patted her back awkwardly. "It was nothing."

Teari grabbed Meg by her shoulders and held her away, wrinkling her nose in disgust. "You stink."

———

Jed and Shay were walking shoulder to shoulder as the group made their way back to the castle.

Teari wanted to feel the fresh air on her hands. It was a strange thing to demand but since she'd spent the past few weeks with no arms below her elbows, no one argued about it.

Chel was there with Klaus, just in case. The forests of Hell weren't completely safe. The dead would come for this group without Meg with them.

Jed's arm itched to wrap around Shay but he didn't want the others to dwell on it. They'd done their best to skirt the details of their relationship. Jed didn't want word to spread, he didn't want a target on Shay's back.

The chatter of the group was interrupted by the heavy *clop-clop-clop* of hooves.

Shay turned and focused on the figure in the distance. It was coming toward them.

"What's that?" Teari asked. "Is that... is that a horse?"

"Stay here," Chel said. "I'll go check it out."

Chel moved to take flight, but Shay held out a hand to stop him.

"Wait. I think I know who that is." Shay walked away from the group, closer to the oncoming figure. She recognized the glint of his onyx coat, the sheen that soaked up every wavelength of visible light. He was fast–a blur at times–but then, his motion glitched and he stumbled.

"Nero?" Shay shouted. "Nero, is that you?"

"No," Jed warned. "Don't, Shay, he's not your horse anymore." Jed grabbed for Shay's arm to stop her from moving closer.

"That's ridiculous. He's fine. He's just bigger." Shay moved closer.

Klaus squinted at the horse moving toward them. "That's the biggest damn horse I've ever seen in my life." He looked at Shay. "That's your horse?"

Shay nodded. "His name is Nero. But, he's changed. He rescued me from a Crossroads Demon–"

"Oh, shit." Chel exclaimed as he moved protectively in front of Shay. "That's not just a horse."

Shay shoved at Chel. Jed tugged her backward. "Will you two leave me alone? It's just my horse!" Shay complained.

Nero slowed, his gallop becoming uneven. His head dipped lower and lower toward the road. He went down on one knee, hooves scraped against the asphalt, slipping. He collapsed before he could reach them, his sides heaving as he breathed heavily.

"Nero!" Shay shoved at Chel and Jed and ran toward the horse. She dropped to her knees and touched his face.

Nero's giant black eyes focused on her. He was in pain and exhausted. She wondered if something had been chasing him. Shay looked down the road but saw nothing in the distance.

"Are you hurt, boy?" Shay asked, petting Nero's cheek and the wide space between his ears. She inspected the gold ring in his ear and the gold chain that looped down to another chain around his neck.

"That's not just a horse, Shay," Klaus warned. "That there is a Crossroads Demon."

"He's my horse," Shay said, panic rising in her chest. "I've had him since he was a baby. Something is wrong with him."

Chel laughed. "He's a Demon, Shay. There's plenty wrong with him now. We got to get him out of here."

"No!" Tears were collecting in Shay's eyes. "He saved me more than once. Whatever is wrong with him, I have to help."

Teari was circling the giant horse, inspecting the side of him that was up. "He's injured." She pointed to the bright red wound on his flank that was oozing inky liquid.

"Oh no." Shay ran her hands over his face and neck, down his back and front legs looking for more injuries. "What happened to you?" she asked.

Nero didn't answer. Not that he could but Shay still felt the need to speak to him as though he could communicate in her language.

Teari was kneeling near the wound on Nero's flank, her hand hovering over it. Nero's muscles twitched and he whinnied weakly.

"I can't fix this," Teari said. "This is a Demon talon injury."

"What does that mean?" Shay asked.

"There's usually poison." Teari bit her lip as she thought for a moment. She held up a finger and pointed toward the castle. "A basilisk can fix this. And Meg just happens to have a tank full of them."

"What's a basilisk?" Shay asked.

"It looks like a snake but they have many uses and

they're unique to Hell." Teari stood and looked at the two Hellions. "We need to get Nero back to Meg's stables."

Klaus laughed. "That beast must weigh four thousand pounds. I can't lift it."

Chel crossed his arms. "I don't approve of bringing a Crossroads Demon back to Meg's land. It's too dangerous."

"Nero is not dangerous," Shay argued.

Chel shook his head.

"It's not a good idea," Jed said, touching Shay's back.

Anger rose in Shay's chest. Her fingertips tingled as emotion flooded her body. "I'm not leaving him here in the road, half dead. He deserves better than that." Shay sat down in the road. "I'll just stay here with him until he's better."

There was a long silence as tears dripped down Shay's cheeks. She leaned against Nero and rubbed his neck like she used to do on the ranch when their lives were very different. She remembered the day she'd found him, covered in bee stings and half dead. She didn't carry him back to the ranch and nurse him back to life just to have him die in the road like this. No, it wouldn't do. Shay would stay with him and find another way, even if it was without everyone's help.

Klaus left. Shay watched his large figure shrink to the

size of a pin head in the sky as he made his way to the castle.

Jed crouched next to Shay. "This is craziness, Shay-baby." His words were barely a whisper. "We can't save him."

"You could do something." Shay glared at Jed. "He crossed the Veil after Clyburn dragged me to Hell. *He* saved *me*." Shay pointed her finger, accusingly. "You could do something, anything right now."

Jed sighed, rose to his feet, and moved to inspect the wound. He glanced at Teari.

"You healed my stitched face," Shay reminded Jed.

"That was different. There was no Demon poison involved." Jed held his hand over Nero's wound and shook his head. "I can't, Shay. I can't make this worse. I haven't come across anything like this before." A hollowness filled his gut as he realized he couldn't do a thing to help Nero. It made him feel like dog shit. Jed would do anything for Shay. But he wouldn't risk fucking up healing Nero. If Nero died because of Jed, he knew Shay would never forgive him.

Teari touched Jed's arm. "The basilisk will fix it. We just have to get him there." She motioned to the castle.

"Maybe we should go get the basilisk and bring it here?" Jed asked.

"You guys can go," Shay said. "I'll wait here."

Jed glanced to Chel who was pacing near Shay. The Hellion was a bit too protective of her and it worried Jed. It made him wonder if he should lay some claim in Shay publicly so the Hellion would back the fuck off.

"Do you know what you are?" Teari asked Jed, her hand still on his arm.

Jed turned to face her. "Yeah. I know."

"The blue is very pretty." Teari was inspecting the aura around Jed. "Is it always glowing?"

"Usually," Jed said. He didn't want to talk about himself, especially toward a pure-blood Angel. "Are you going to try and kill me now?" he asked. "That's what your kind typically does next."

Teari shook her head. "No. No you brought back Nightingale and she's family. I could never kill you." Teari patted Jed's arm before moving away from him. She whispered, "You should do something about her," she motioned to Shay. "She's quite spectacular and I've noticed a few lingering gazes." Teari looked at Chel.

Jed rubbed his face. Wonderful, now he was going to have to fight a Hellion to lay claim to his girl. The fun was never ending on any realm.

The fading sunlight was blocked out and a large shadow covered the road. Everyone looked up.

"Oh good," Chel said. "She's here."

"What's that?" Shay asked, covering Nero with her

upper body as though she could protect him from the giant shadow that was approaching.

Chel held out a hand to help her up. "It's Clea. She transforms into that giant bird. The argentavis." He tugged Shay away from Nero.

Jed and Teari moved away from Nero as well.

"Clea can carry him to the stables," Chel said.

Clea swooped down and gently grabbed Nero's lifeless body with her claws. She faltered under his weight, flapping her wings harder to get back in the air.

Breath caught in Shay's throat as she feared Clea would drop Nero. She didn't though. Her giant wings beat *one-two-three*, and she took off into the sky, headed toward the castle, veering from side to side every so often under the weight of the horse.

"Let's go," Jed moved closer to Shay and led her away from Chel. "We can meet Nero there if we walk fast enough."

"I can fly and carry her back," Chel offered. "It would be faster than walking."

"No," Jed said.

Shay's mouth was open, ready to say something but from the worry lines creasing Jed's forehead, she decided not to.

"It's fine, we can walk," Shay said as she glanced over

her shoulder at the others. "You all can fly back if you want."

"We'll walk too," Chel said sternly. "Just in case there are any more surprises."

———

NERO DIDN'T WAKE when Noah brought in the basket with the basilisk.

Shay was kneeling next to Nero, petting him gently and whispering to him.

"I hate touching these things," Noah complained as he opened the basket. He reached in and after a few attempts grabbed the creature inside. Shay's eyes went wide as he pulled out the snake-like creature with sharp teeth.

"Are you sure?" Shay asked, looking to Teari.

"Yes." Teari nodded. "It's worked on other poison injuries. Meg had a cut on her arm that's been healing up nicely."

Noah lined up the basilisk with the wound on Nero's flank. The creature wiggled and struggled against Noah's hold. Thick slime dripped onto the hay where Nero was sleeping.

Nero didn't move when the basilisk latched onto the wound. Noah held it in place, crouching to get in a comfortable position.

"How long do I have to hold this thing?" Noah asked.

"Until it releases," Teari replied.

The basilisk stayed latched for a good ten minutes before releasing Nero's flank. The creature sagged in Noah's hands as though it were a sated infant. Noah tucked the basilisk in the basket and stood. "Well, my work here is done." He joked.

"We need to do this three times a day." Teari was inspecting the wound that was still red but weeping considerably less. "This thing has festered for a long time. It's probably gone to his bloodstream." Teari touched the sensitive skin around the wound. "At least he's not in as much pain now." Teari made her way out of the horse stall. "He needs rest."

"Come on," Jed helped Shay stand. "Let him rest. We'll come back later."

"You all should get cleaned up," Noah said as they left the barn. "We are having a party tonight in the ballroom. There's going to be music and dancing and pizza!"

FOURTEEN

The castle ballroom was exquisite. Dark etched wood and forest green wallpaper stretched several floors up to a cavernous ceiling. A wall of windows looked over Hell with an expanse of balconies and open glass doors to let in the cool night air. Dark curtains billowed in the breeze. Lightning was illuminating dark Hellsky in the distance.

Noah was standing at a record player, twirling a record between his palms. "I haven't heard this tune in ages." He set the record in place and adjusted the needle arm, then turned up the volume. *Pump up the Jam* started playing. Noah broke out in ridiculous exaggerated dance, pumping his arms and hips in motion with the beat.

Nightingale stopped spinning with baby Thrush in her arms and made a face. "This isn't music," she said as she skated over to Noah. The music was too loud to hear what she was saying to him as she thumbed through a stack of records. She pulled out a record and tapped it.

With a face of disappointment, Noah changed the record and *Flashdance* started playing.

"These people have something for the eighties," Shay whispered to Jed.

Jed was drinking cold beer for the first time in years. He'd never felt relaxed enough to let his guard down, but tonight seemed worthy. What could happen in a castle in Hell? There was plenty of protection.

"It was decent music," Jed said. His fingers were tapping on the table.

Shay watched his fingers. Jed had rolled up the sleeves of his dress shirt. The muscles of his lower arms flexed, strong and developed from decades of spell casting.

"You want something to eat?" Jed asked Shay, motioning to the table spread with pizza and snacks.

Shay shook her head. "I'm too worried about Nero to eat."

Jed leaned closer. "He's going to be okay. Teari is a healer."

The ballroom doors opened and handful of people walked in. Meg was wearing a tight, low cut black dress. Jed paused his table tapping and his hand flew to his neck, rubbing the scars from her bite.

Shay was watching him closely. Whatever had happened between Jed and Meg was before her time. But it had left a lasting impression on him. Still, it was easy to see he didn't trust Meg, he was easy to tell her when she'd gone too far, when she'd done something outrageous. Being the ruler of Hell, Meg never seemed to get upset with Jed, it was as though she allowed him to work out his frustrations with her as payment for what she'd done to him.

Shay wanted to rest her head on Jed's shoulder and watch the lightning display outside. She'd always loved watching the storms travel across the Montana flats. She turned away from Meg and Klaus dancing. Everyone was dancing. Nightingale twirled with Thrush in her arms, Noah grabbed her hand and spun them back to him. Thrush giggled and drooled. Everyone looked so normal, Shay could barely believe she was in Hell. She glanced at Jed, wishing he'd ask her to dance. She could sense his reserve. While they'd spent plenty of nights together wrapped up in each other, when the daylight came, he was distant.

Shay shuddered and rubbed her arms. She should have brought a jacket.

After Meg and Klaus finish dancing to *Time of My Life*, Meg made her way to the balcony.

Shay didn't trust her. Meg still seemed off, after everything that happened. Everyone else seemed to forgive her for stealing Thrush in the night and taking him to the Seven Kingdoms of Heaven for baptism. Shay realized that these people had history, one that she didn't quite understand or fit into. She rubbed her arm absently. She was the only human here in a realm she didn't belong in or know much about. She'd felt comfortable at the chapel in the graveyard for the weeks that they were there. Now everything was in upheaval. They'd been moved back to the suite in the castle. And while Jed had shared a bed with her at the chapel, he'd set his bags down in the opposite bedroom after they'd entered the suite.

Suddenly, Meg ran out of the room, holding a hand over her mouth like she was going to be sick.

Noah watched, a grim gaze on his face. Nightingale tugged at Noah's arm, redirecting him to dance more.

Teari calmly walked out of the room, following Meg.

"What do you think is wrong with her?" Shay asked Jed.

"She probably ate too much." Jed sipped at his beer.

Shay followed Jed's gaze; he was watching Chel on the other side of the room. Shay wondered why. The Hellion was nice and more than a few times had discussed survival gear and hunting knives with her. It was hard to come across people who could hold those discussions that weren't a little conspiratorial in nature.

Chel turned and looked at Shay quickly before looking

away again and continuing his conversation with the Hellion named Tukka.

Jed's chair slid back and he stood abruptly.

"What's wrong?" Shay asked.

"I need some air. Stay here." Jed's pace was brisk as he walked to the balcony.

Shay was worried about Nero. It was dark outside and he was alone and injured in an unknown place. Shay didn't feel like sitting any longer, she stood and made her way out of the ballroom.

FIFTEEN

Shay went to the suite to grab her jacket. She found a thick flannel with lambswool on the inside. She decided to take her pistol as well, and a knife for good measure. She glanced at her empty bed then moved the pillows to make it appear a body was sleeping there. Whatever was up with Jed, she wasn't going to bother him. She was just going to let him assume she'd left the party and gone to sleep.

As she left the suite, she couldn't stop dwelling on Jed's strange actions tonight. He'd promised that she wouldn't be alone. He'd promised to be with her but tonight he seemed so distant. There was something going on with him and she was disappointed that he wouldn't tell her.

Shay made her way to the door of the castle, surprised with how easily it opened for her. The door was solid wood, marred from eons of use. She walked across the courtyard headed for the stables, thankful for the little bit of lighting along the walk way.

Near the forest, she could see Hellions on patrol. Since Meg had stolen Thrush in the night, Shay had noticed more Hellions than when they'd first arrived.

Shay made her way to the stables. She hadn't been completely alone since she'd arrived in Hell. There was always someone nearby, always someone watching her. There was freedom in being alone–an autonomy that she enjoyed. The night breeze was cold and Shay could see her breath. She hoped Nero wasn't cold.

———

NERO WAS SLEEPING in the same position they'd left him. Shay entered the stall and curled next to him, her hand on his side. She'd always felt comfortable hanging out with Nero on the ranch. Whenever there was a problem or she was upset, she could be found in his stall. Nero had comforted her plenty of times after one of Clyburn's incidents. Shay wished she could give Nero the same comfort.

Shay laid her head on Nero's shoulder and closed her eyes, listening to the strong beating of his heart.

The barn door opened and footsteps approached Nero's stall. The sounds of a man struggling with carrying something heavy echoed. The stall door opened and Noah was there with the basilisk in the basket.

"Oh," he smiled when he saw Shay. "I didn't realize you were here."

Shay was leaning against Nero, her hand resting on his neck. "I didn't like the idea of him being alone."

Nero's eyes flashed open and he whinnied softly.

"Glad to see he's awake," Noah said as he opened the basket and reached for the basilisk. The creature wiggled and slimed, its jaws opened in anticipation of Nero's wound.

"It's the first time," Shay said.

Nero noticed the basilisk and spooked. He struggled to get to his feet. He whinnied anxiously and got his front half up.

Shay tried to move away but the stall wall was against her back.

"Whoa. Whoa," Noah said as he maneuvered the basilisk. "Settle down, boy." He was quick to get the basilisk to latch onto the wound.

Nero lost it when he felt the basilisk on his wound. He stumbled, dragged his back end a few feet before falling again. Then he was still.

"Knocked yourself out did you?" Noah asked the horse.

It happened so fast. Shay was trying to soothe Nero

but the giant horse didn't have his wits about him. Shay had been pressed against the side of the stall edging her way out but then Nero fell, his ribs pressed against her. She shoved at him as he slid, nearly crushing her. His belly hit her knee, dragging her down with him. He was too heavy to move, and Shay cried out when she felt the bone of her leg flex too far. There was a loud crack as Nero landed. *Snap*. Her femur broke in half.

"Ah!" Shay cried, her back pressed against the wall of the stall.

Noah's head jerked in Shay's direction. "Oh no!" Noah was looking between the basilisk and Shay. "Shit."

"Move." Shay pushed at Nero, biting her lip against the pain in her right leg.

Noah didn't want to lose the basilisk.

"Let it finish," Shay said, bracing herself against the hard floor. She wanted Nero to get better. Ten minutes wouldn't fix her broken leg. "Just, let it finish," Shay said the last word as an exhale, fighting the searing pain. She rubbed her hip and pressed her fingers between Nero and her trapped leg. When she pulled it back, it was covered in blood. "Oh god." Shay took a shuddered breath and wiped her hand on her jacket. "It's going to be fine. It's going to be fine." She chanted to herself.

Sixteen

Noah put the basilisk in the basket then moved around the side of Nero to get a good look at Shay's predicament.

"Damn," Noah rubbed his chin. "This is going to hurt like a bitch."

"You can move him?" Shay asked, panting in pain. She'd never felt anything so excruciating.

"A crushed leg and a broken bone." Noah rubbed his hands together. "I won't be gentle. We're moving this beast then I'm picking you up and running." He nodded. "It's going to hurt."

"Okay," Shay agreed, breathless. "Do what you have to do."

Noah called on his Astral magic. He moved Nero, lifting him and shoving him to the side.

"Don't hurt him!" Shay reached toward Nero.

She was free. Bone stuck through the rip in her pants and her leg was surrounded by blood.

"Time to go," Noah said, gathering her into his arms. "There's just one problem."

"What's that?"

"Hellions drink blood. I have to move faster than them." He gripped Shay tightly against his chest, then he ran.

Noah ran so fast it knocked the wind out of Shay. By the time they exited the barn, she was unconscious.

Noah was a blur as he moved. But, he could hear the Hellion new recruits sniffing out the fresh blood. They couldn't help it. At least three of them were running behind him, eager for a taste?. They hadn't learned control yet.

Noah made it to the front door and kicked it open. The slam echoed. Everyone in the castle had to have heard it.

The Hellion lair opened and Klaus ran out.

Noah didn't give him time to speak. "Get Teari to the infirmary right now!"

Noah kept running, down long dark hallways and up a set of winding stairs. He cursed whoever thought to put the infirmary at the farthest point from the front door.

Noah set Shay down on one of the cots. She was pale but still breathing.

Teari ran in with Klaus at her side.

"What happened?" Teari began inspecting Shay's leg.

"The Demon horse fell on her." Noah was cutting off her pants with a pair of medic scissors. "She was trapped for about ten minutes while the basilisk was on Nero's wound."

"Why didn't you stop the basilisk?" Teari asked, her hands hovering over Shay's leg.

"She told me not to." Noah threw the bloodied pieces of Shay's pants aside. "Damn girl cares more about that horse than most people." He turned to Klaus. "Three new recruits were following us. I'm sure there's a blood trail."

Klaus nodded, knowing. "I'll take care of it," he said as he ran out of the room. The new recruits couldn't get a taste for fresh blood, especially Shay's human blood–it would send them into a frenzy.

"She's going to need a transfusion," Nightingale said to Noah. "Can you get some from storage?"

Noah disappeared. There was a large storage refrigerator in the kitchen to stock the Hellion's with bagged blood. Noah never considered it could be of use for a time like this.

———

"WHAT HAPPENED?" Jed ran into the room, worry plastered on his face. His aura illuminated in Teari's presence.

"She broke her leg." Teari was connecting blood tubing to an I.V. in Shay's arm. "I healed the bone but her leg was crushed. She needed blood."

Jed pushed up his sleeves as he moved closer. He touched Shay's face. "Where was she found?"

"She was visiting Nero." Teari's hands glowed with a white light as she focused her healing energy over Shay's leg. "The horse fell on her."

"Fuck." Jed rubbed his hands together. "Let me help. I've healed her before." He pulled up his sleeves. "Never anything this extensive though."

Teari nodded, appreciating the assistance. "I'll help you if you need it," she said.

It had barely been a day since her arms grew back and she felt rusty. Healing humans was precarious, they died quicker than Angels and Demons. Teari didn't have a moment to waste and she'd already spent enough time starting the blood transfusion. There was internal bleeding and ruptured muscle to fix before it was too late and Shay never walked correctly again.

Jed whispered words that sounded like a good promise. Like a sunset over the lake. Like a humming prayer.

"You're good at this," Teari said, glancing up. "That

aura though." She shook her head in concern. "How did you ever hide that on the Earthen plane?"

Jed nodded, knowing his aura was glowing strong. He was using every magical store in his bones to help heal Shay. He'd never forgive himself if he didn't give his all.

"The runes helped," Jed broke his chanting to reply. "But if I used too much, an Angel or Demon would show up ready to kill. It's nothing but a beacon."

Teari moved her hands toward Shay's knee, focusing on the damaged ligaments and bone cracks. "She's going to be out for a few days. This isn't an overnight healing. If she were on the Earthen plane right now, she'd lose her leg."

Jed nodded, knowing. "She's fragile."

Teari smiled, remembering. "I thought the same once. But humans are strong in many ways." She winked at Jed. "You'll find out eventually."

Jed focused on healing Shay. He knit together a leaking artery, torn ligaments in her hip, a crack in her pelvic bone. His hands moved over her pelvis and he strengthened that and her hip, sensing the torn tissue on the left side. It could be an old injury. A fall off a horse or something that happened during childhood.

"You care for her," Teari said.

Jed was about to reply but the door to the infirmary opened. He glanced over his shoulder as Chel entered the room.

Chel growled in Jed's direction as he stood at the end of the bed. "She lost a lot of blood."

"I know," Teari nodded. "It's being replaced."

"Noah said she broke her leg." Chel motioned to the red scar across her thigh. He turned to Jed. "Where were you?"

"I was here." Jed didn't want to argue with the Hellion, but the dude was overstepping and pissing him off.

"Answer me," Chel demanded.

Teari cleared her throat. "Maybe you two should take this discussion in the hallway. You're distracting."

Jed's aura dimmed as he glared at Chel and stomped toward the door.

Seventeen

"I'm not sure what the fuck you think you're doing," Jed growled at Chel as soon as the door to the infirmary closed.

"I could say the same about you." Chel took a step closer.

"What the fuck are you doing here. She doesn't need you."

Chel laughed. "Really?"

"If you want a girlfriend, go find one of your own kind." Jed pointed down the hall. "She's not available."

"I don't want to date her," Chel scoffed. "She's human. A tiny, weak, defenseless human," Chel said with disgust.

"I don't believe you," Jed argued. "You are always near her. You just show up out of the blue."

"Look at me," he roared. "I'd crush her. I'd break her in half. I'm not that fucked in the head, you half-breed idiot." Chel jabbed a finger at Jed. "I don't trust *you* with her. She deserves better."

"What's so wrong with me?" Jed paused. Magic was swelling in his fingertips as anger overtook him. He was ready to blast this bastard with something like he'd given Alastor. He was sure that would get him kicked out of Meg's castle though. He did his best to control it.

"Fucking lay claim to her. She smells only faintly of you but you never touch her. You're too distant. She deserves better than that. There's a mistrust between you both. And you can't be living in a place like Hell with no faith in each other. This is too dangerous." Chel glared at Jed. "I've seen far too many females of my kind lost to the terrors of Hell. Shay doesn't deserve that. She is innocent." Chel poked a finger at Jed's head. "I know you're still considering it. Taking her memories and sending her back to the Earthen plane to die alone on that Montana ranch."

Jed blinked.

"The Hellions are still under orders to protect her. And you. Meg demanded it. But I don't trust you to protect her. I'm not completely convinced she doesn't need protection *from* you."

Jed was feeling like shit. Chel wasn't wrong. Jed had been struggling with Shay. He wanted her so badly but he wanted her to be safe. He'd made promises and broken them. He'd lied to her. That night she woke to him casting a spell on her memories, it was to wipe her mind of everything that had happened. And he'd hated himself for attempting, he hated that she'd woken up in the middle of it, he hated that he'd lied to her about what he was actually doing. Clara raised him better than that but somewhere along his lifetime, he'd disappointed her memory.

"You better figure yourself the fuck out," Chel said. "Or I'll get her a room in the Hellion barracks. I don't trust you sleeping next to her every night."

"We sleep in separate rooms." It was a half-truth. Jed rubbed his face, wishing he'd learn to shut the fuck up.

Chel laughed. It was a wicked sound. "See. That's your problem, you little fuck. She should be next to you every night. But you don't trust yourself." Chel paced in frustration. "It's you or me. I will not have her fall victim to the creatures of Hell or the new Hellion recruits we've been bringing in." He held up three large fingers. "And now three of them have gotten a taste of her blood. I can't guarantee that they won't come looking for more."

"She's mine." Jed's fingertips flashed with blue sparks.

"Oh, now you give a shit." Chel laughed. "Where the fuck were you when her leg was getting crushed under that giant Demon horse?"

"You piece of shit..." Sparks flew from Jed's fingers as he punched Chel in the jaw.

Chel didn't move. He barely flinched at Jed's assault. He shifted his stance, bracing himself for a fight. "Let's do it, shithead half-breed." Chel grabbed his blade and threw it aside. "I'll just use my fists." He cracked his knuckles. "Promise."

Jed had never fought a Hellion before, but he'd fought other giant Demons in his time. They were all the same. Brute strength and stupid.

Chel's fists were twice the size of Jed's, but that didn't stop him from throwing the first punch. Jed's wrist made a terrible sound as it bounced off Chel's jaw.

Chel didn't move, only smirked. Tension crackled between them. Chel squared his shoulders, his uniform stretching against muscle and the glint of resolve in his eyes. "That's all you got?"

Jed made a swift gesture with his hands, conjuring swirling tendrils of iridescent energy that crackled in the air.

Chel held up his open hands. "I got rid of my weapon. Leave yours." His muscles tensed, preparing for Jed's assault.

"No." Jed's arcane energies swirled into a vortex, aiming to disorient and immobilize Chel. He chose violence.

Chel dodged the tendrils of energy, narrowly evading the attack. He dropped to the ground, rolled with surprising agility, and grabbed the blade he'd tossed aside. The blade sliced through the magical energy, dispersing the tendrils like mist.

Chel lunged forward, his blade gleaming in the dim light.

Jed's fingers twitched, casting battle spells. The air crackled with the clash of steel and the ethereal.

Their fighting echoed through the halls of the castle. A battle was nothing more than Jed's power versus Chel's unwavering determination.

Suddenly a voice shouted down the hallway. "Stop!"

Jed and Chel froze, their eyes meeting in silent understanding. Chel sheathed his blade. Jed shook the energy away from his fingertips.

Skeele approached. "Take this fight outdoors," he growled at the two as though they were boys playing. "You're too loud."

Skeele entered the infirmary without another word.

"I'll refrain from killing you on one condition." Chel smiled, showing sharp teeth.

"What's that?"

"You shut your mouth and let me train her to defend herself."

"She's killed Angels before. She can fight."

"She can fight better," Chel said.

Jed rubbed the overgrown stubble on his face, contemplating. He knew Shay needed training. She could hunt and kill but they were in Hell now. Demons were different creatures. They'd survived the camp in California because there was help and Jed had nearly drained his magic stores fighting. Shay didn't have magic and he knew if she came across a Demon like Alastor again, she'd be dead.

"I'll train her as though I'd train my sister if she were still alive," Chel promised.

"Fine," Jed agreed. "But if I get wind of anything more. I'll kill you."

"I *dare* you." Chel leaned toward Jed, his smile jeering.

Eighteen

The dead were wandering about quietly in the forest behind Jed and Shay. Sticks snapped, leaves rustled, groans interrupted Jed's teaching.

Shay rubbed her sore leg. She'd ventured out against Teari's wishes. She'd been cooped up inside for days. The castle was starting to feel like a prison and Jed's thoughts seemed so far away.

"Let's start with a warm-up exercise," Jed said, showing Shay how to stretch, twist, and tap her fingers into nimbleness.

Shay mimicked Jed's motions, her fingers moving faster and faster to keep up with him.

Jed watched her hands intensely. "That's good." His fingers moved in a rhythm only he seemed to know. He clucked his tongue lightly like a conductor so Shay could

"]

follow along to the beat. After three rounds he started with the first spell. Jed backed up in a circle, looking for the nearest walking corpse to practice on.

"That one," he jerked his chin to a dead man dragging his foot. "Like this." Jed's fingers danced as he cast a spell to freeze the zombie in place.

Shay's fingers followed along in the same dance, the same nimble spellcast. But no energy moved from her hands like it did Jed's.

Shay dropped her shoulders, defeated. "It didn't work." She flexed her fingers.

"Try again."

"I'm too human." Her voice was thick with disappointment.

Jed touched her shoulder. "I won't think less of you," he joked, the corner of his lips tipping up.

Shay swung at him. "You shit." Her fist landed on his bicep, and she moved to smack him again.

"I think you can do it," Jed said as he sprung away from Shay's fist. "You just need more time."

"It's been a long time. It's been forever," Shay exaggerated. She wanted to do something special. Everyone around her had power or wings or super strength. She had nothing.

Jed's eyes went wide and he held a finger to his lips. "Shhh. The dead will hear and come."

Shay paused and looked around. It wasn't long before the shuffling of feet started getting closer. "Shit."

"Let's go." Jed grabbed Shay's arm and tugged her in his direction.

The old Shay would have been pissed for not being asked which direction to run in, but she'd spent enough time with Jed to know that he had a knack for finding a way out. He'd never led her wrong.

Jed and Shay ran through the forest in a roundabout path toward the burning caves.

"Should we go to the cemetery?" Shay asked. "To lose them?"

"We can't risk bringing a horde to Thrush." He ducked under a low branch then held it up for Shay. "If we go back to the burning caves, they'll just wander away. They won't get close. Meg's there. They won't go near her."

"Not like the fast ones did?" Shay asked.

"The fast ones didn't follow the rules of Hell." Jed slowed to check their surroundings. "These slow ones will just move on." He motioned for her to move faster.

Jed and Shay moved quickly through the forest. Once they found the road, they ran parallel to stay hidden. Soon the moans of the walking dead got further and further away. Jed and Shay slowed, only to hear voices not far away. They both came to a stop and listened.

Shay ducked near a fallen tree and focused in the distance. She pointed. Jed crouched near a thick tree trunk coated in lichen and followed her line of sight.

There were three men dressed in black with white collars. Deacons.

Shay tapped her ear. Jed shook his head. Neither could hear what the Deacons were discussing. The dragging footsteps of the dead were getting closer. Jed and Shay were stuck in the middle.

Shay's heart thumped in her chest as they waited. She didn't like the feeling of being trapped. She'd spend too much of her life stuck between safety and the bliss of freedom. She turned to see the decaying forms of the dead as they meandered toward them and estimated how much time they had. At the rate they crept and how easily they were distracted, Shay figured it was less than six minutes before they needed to move again. She focused on the meeting of the Deacons in the road. Hopefully the men in black would be done by then.

———

JED AND SHAY broke through the forest line and right into the Hellion training grounds. Both were running and panting.

The Hellions secured their weapons and let their

guests enter the training fields. Skeele and Chel stopped training.

Jed bent over, hands on his knees. "Damn, I need to run more." He wiped perspiration off his brow. "Been a long time. Too long." He patted his stomach. "Getting comfortable is never a good thing."

Shay coughed. "I was kind of enjoying not running for my life on a daily basis." Shay rubbed her right leg. It was sore and while Teari and Jed had healed her, there were still strange aches that she got when she pushed herself too hard.

"Why were you running?" Skeele asked as he sheathed his blade before crossing his arms and looking down at the human and Nephilim.

"We were training in the forest, past the cemetery and a horde came," Jed said.

"They don't move that fast," Chel said.

Jed held up his hand as he said, "As we were leaving, we found three Deacons in the road not far from here. We had to wait for them to leave. The dead caught up."

"Deacons?" Chel's brows rose in attention.

"Did you hear what the Deacons were saying?" Skeele asked.

"No," Jed shook his head. "We can show you where they were."

Skeele nodded and motioned for Chel to follow.

They hadn't left a single thing behind, not even a footprint. But the Hellions did a thorough job of surveying the area and back to the crossroads.

"Did they have a vehicle?" Skeele asked Jed.

"Not that we saw." Jed did his best to help but he wasn't trained in tracking, only running and hiding.

"You have a spell or something that could help us gain some insight?" Tukka asked.

Jed thought for a moment before reaching into his pocket to pull out the ages old notebook he carried with him. "I might have something. Let me look."

Shay stood close, watching Skeele as he searched. The Hellion Commander had always been hulking and intimidating, but today he seemed gaunt and bony.

Skeele caught her eye more than a handful of times before he finally walked over to her and asked, "What?"

"You seem different," Shay said.

"Nothing's changed." Skeele ran a hand over his head and horns as one runs their hands through their hair in frustration.

"Sure." Shay stepped closer to Jed.

"Why do you ask?" Skeele said.

"You seem tired or sick, and you've lost a lot of weight. You're the Commander of the Hellions." Shay lowered her voice. "Maybe you should see that healer, Teari."

"Not necessary." Skeele walked away from the human and continued on his searching until Jed cleared his throat.

"I found something." He motioned to Skeele and Tukka. "It's a spell that can rewind time but only for a few moments."

Chel watched from a distance.

Jed's fingers tapped and twisted as he chanted the spell, motioning in the area of the road where they'd seen the Deacons.

Transparent leaves rolled across the road before the images of the three Deacons appeared. They were see-through and faded, like Clea's wavering image. Ghosts of the past. Skeele moved closer and watched their lips as they spoke.

"Dead Newcomers."

"Her condition."

"Unlawful."

"What did they say?" Tukka asked.

"What kind of a mess did Meg get herself into now?" Jed asked.

NINETEEN

MEG HAD BEEN MISSING for weeks. No one had told Jed or Shay until a few days ago. Now everyone had collected at the chapel in the graveyard to discuss a plan. Without Meg present, there was risk that Hell would digress into chaos.

"He's found her," Nightingale told the others at the table. "I didn't approach her in the dream. She hasn't slept in a long time."

"Let her sleep," Noah said, shifting a sleeping Thrush in his arms. There was a wet drool mark on his shoulder.

"How long will it take Skeele to bring her back?" Shay asked.

Jed was in the middle of updating the runes on her arms, with real ink this time since the paint didn't last. Shay's blowtorch blue hair contrasted against her pale skin and dark clothing in a newly shortened haircut to her chin. Shay sucked in a breath as Jed tattooed deep over bone.

"Sorry," he said as his thumb rubbed her skin to soothe.

Rumors were starting. Someone had destroyed portals on the Earthen plane. The Deacons had already come knocking on the doors of the burning caves. Clea distracted them and sent them away. But it wasn't enough. The new Hellions had mouths that spoke freely at whatever post they were stationed. They were instructed to bring the rumors back to Klaus and Chel, but some had loose lips and spread their own rumors. The demons of Hell knew the throne was unseated. Meg wasn't as visible as she had been.

There was a knock on the door.

Nightingale moved to answer it. Chel, Klaus, and Tukka entered the room. Suddenly the chapel in the cemetery felt very small.

Klaus was carrying a bag. "This should be everything."

Nightingale took the bag as Jed stopped his tattooing, wiped Shay's skin, and rubbed a layer of healing balm over the fresh ink.

"Are you ready?" Jed asked Shay.

Shay nodded and stood. Her stomach felt queasy. She felt extremely out of place in this realm and she was about to do something crazy.

Tukka grunted in disapproval. "They are nothing alike. This will not work."

Nightingale pulled clothing from the bag and held them up to Shay. "The clothes will fit."

"Her hair is blue," Tukka motioned to Shay's hair. "Meg's is black. Everyone will know it's not her. She doesn't even have Meg's tattoos."

"Or her attitude," Klaus said with a smile, trying to lighten the mood.

"Hush, all of you." Noah patted Thrush's back, soothing him to sleep again. "She has a few of the tattoos. Jed still has time to add more."

"Or we could try the paint again?" Jed suggested, knowing that Shay was hesitant to ink her skin.

"They didn't last." Shay shook her head. "It won't work."

"Here," Nightingale thrust the clothing into Shay's hands. "Go change."

"Come with me." Shay tugged at Jed's shirt as she headed to the bedroom.

Shay closed the door behind Jed and listened to the chatter in the living room.

"They don't want me to do this." Shay tossed the clothing onto the bed and kicked off her boots.

"It doesn't matter." Jed turned his back like a gentleman. "We have to do something until we can get Meg back where she belongs."

"What if she never comes back?" Shay asked. "I'm a human. I am not whatever magical creatures you all are. I don't have wings or magic or battle training."

"Meg doesn't have any of those either." Jed pressed his ear to the wooden door to hear the others speaking.

"She has something that keeps you all in check." Shay pulled on a pair of jeans that were a little too tight on the butt. She changed her shirt to the wide-necked blue T-shirt of Meg's. "Okay. Turn around. Tell me how bad this is."

Jed turned and walked a circle around Shay. "I think this could work." He stopped in front of Shay and frowned.

"It's the blue hair, isn't it?"

Jed shook his head in defeat. "Everyone knows you have the blue hair. We have to hide it."

"It took a really long time to get this shade just right." Shay was annoyed. "If you fuck it up…"

Jed's lip tipped to form a half smile. "Say it like Meg would."

Shay closed her eyes and took a deep breath, collecting every speck of attitude and edge in her person. "If you fuck it up, I will drain you dry." Shay opened her eyes.

Jed was nodding in approval. "That was pretty good." He held out his hands and his fingers danced in rhythmic spellcasting. "Let's just add a little glamour so as not to fuck up your blue."

When Shay left the bedroom, the visitors in the living room were silent, judging, and one of them eating crow, figuratively.

"Fine," Tukka said, his tone dull. "But don't let anyone get too close to her. Meg has blue eyes."

"We will make sure," Klaus said, reaching for the door handle so they could leave.

Chel motioned for Shay to follow them. "After you, Queen of Hell."

TWENTY

SHAY STOOD in the middle of Meg's room feeling uneasy. "This seems so wrong," she said.

Jed was brushing crushed bird seed off the balcony railing.

"What's this?" Shay picked up the jar of mottled feathers from Meg's bedside table.

"I'm not sure," Jed said as he walked into the room. "But judging from the scarce decorations in this room, if it's here then it's important to her."

Shay set the jar down and wandered around the room, then the closet, then the bathroom. "Do I have to stay in here?" she asked. "It really feels like a violation of her privacy."

Jed followed Shay. "Look, we are doing her a favor."

"No one will know." Shay made her way to the balcony for some fresh air.

Jed stood next to her, scanning the tree line. He saw movement and pointed it out to Shay. "That creature would know if this room were empty."

Shay leaned forward and squinted. "What is it?"

"Probably a demon."

"You don't think it's Demore?" Shay asked.

Jed shook his head. "It's too early in the night for Demore." He took a piece of sharp charcoal from his jacket pocket and began sketching runes of protection on the balcony railing. "It could be another Deacon."

"Meg drinks blood," Shay said. "Are they going to want me to drink blood?"

"You don't have to drink blood. You're human."

There was a cry off in the forest. It sounded like an animal or a bird. But Jed and Shay knew it could be something else.

Shay's breasts felt warm as milk letdown. Her body thought the sounds was a baby.

"Ugh." Shay touched her chest and felt wetness. "Is this ever going to stop?" She knew it could go on for weeks while her milk dried up. Now that Nightingale was back, Thrush didn't need a wet nurse.

Jed touched her arm. "Come inside, I'll help you with that."

"Are you going to try the reverse spell again?" Shay asked, wincing. "It kinda hurt."

Jed closed the balcony doors and brought her to the bathroom. He closed and locked the door.

"Can you do something so it doesn't hurt this time?" Shay asked, nervous. She was glad she could help Thrush but she didn't think she'd ever put herself through that experience again.

Jed turned to Shay, moving close. He wrapped his arms around her, rubbed her back before his hands traveled down to her thighs and he lifted her onto the counter.

Jed reached for the hem of her shirt, pulling it up.

"What are you doing?" Shay asked, warmth curling in her abdomen.

"I think I know what went wrong last time." He pulled her shirt off then reached for her bra, unclipping it.

"What went wrong?"

"The milk was stuck." He kissed her neck.

"In my boobs?" Shay giggled.

"Um hm." Jed's mouth trailed across her collarbone and down the front of her chest.

"Oh my gosh, you're not going to–"

Jed's mouth covered her nipple and she felt the sensation of a gentle tug. He drained her then whispered a spell that sounded like the gentlest lapping of the ocean.

"Did it hurt this time?" he asked.

Shay shook her head, the warmth that had pooled in her abdomen had turned to fire. She reached for his jeans and tugged him closer. "You're going to have to finish what you started."

"Anything for my queen," Jed said with the quirk of his lips.

It had been days and days since they'd last been together. Jed was hesitant to touch her after she'd nearly been crushed in the stables. Her leg had healed but Jed's emotions remained buoyant after Chel's demands to lay claim to Shay. And now she was a body double for Meg. Things had gone from bad to worse. Jed couldn't get caught being handsy with the Queen of Hell. That was Skeele's job. Anger seethed under Jed's skin as he thought of Skeele touching Shay.

"What's wrong?" Shay asked, her fingers tracing the planes of his abdomen.

"I was just thinking." Jed ran a hand through his hair.

"Stop thinking." Shay leaned forward to kiss him, wanting more after he lit the flame inside her with his mouth a few moments ago. "Please stop thinking."

He leaned into her kiss, devouring her mouth. Nimble fingers made quick work of removing her jeans. Jed rubbed her thighs, his fingers touching the scars on her right leg.

Shay flinched. The scar was tender, but the memories

it brought back were worse. Nero was still comatose, even after all of the basilisk treatments.

Jed's fingers moved to her core, rubbing against the thin fabric.

Shay made small noises as he stroked her.

The scar on his neck pinched. He opened his eyes and saw Meg on the countertop. Jed froze, pulling away. "I'm sorry." He cleared his throat and adjusted Shay's shirt.

"What's wrong?"

It was too much. Jed didn't want to hurt her. He was at a loss. Chel's threats were echoing between his ears. He saw her scar, the fear in her eyes. He'd done this to her. If he'd just left her alone and never followed her to that ranch she'd be home and safe. She wouldn't be in the middle of this shit show with him.

"Jed?" Shay searched his face.

He didn't answer because they were soon interrupted by two Hellions looking to escort Shay/Meg to watch the new recruits get their uniforms at the training barracks.

TWENTY-ONE

NOAH VISITED JED AND SHAY, interrupting a perfectly serene breakfast on the balcony. Noah sat between them, crossed his hands over his stomach and leaned his head back. "Ah, it's so quiet here. I forgot what silence was like. No baby babble. No Nightingale asking me to go find diapers. No Meg demanding waffles." Noah took in an exaggerated deep breath. "I could sit here all day and enjoy the silence."

Jed's fork clattered against the plate as it dropped. "Except you can't."

"What?" Noah laughed. "You don't want me hanging around as a third wheel?" Noah looked back and forth at Jed and Shay. "Bullies."

"We really love having you around, Noah," Shay said, patting Noah's hand. "It's just..."

"You'd rather walk around naked and screw like rabbits all day?" Noah dead panned.

"Dude," Jed leaned forward.

"Men are such pigs." Shay took a sip of her coffee and shook her head, wishing it were true.

"Don't talk like that around her," Jed said.

"I grew up on a ranch, I've heard worse," Shay said.

"You shouldn't have to." Jed took a bite of bacon.

"Welp, seems I've outlived my welcome this morning." Noah stood. "I just stopped by to tell you that we've found Meg. She's in a Safe House. I need you two to go visit her. We're trying to keep her spirits up until we can figure out what the Deacons want." Noah's hand lingered on the balcony railing. "You know, there's lots of birds here. If you put a little seed on the railing they'll visit."

"Maybe you could bring us some," Shay suggested.

"My time here is done." Noah smirked before disappearing.

Shay looked at Jed. "I guess he doesn't want to be bothered with running errands for me."

"What do you need?" Jed asked. "I can get it for you."

Shay shook her head and wiped her mouth with a napkin. She was thinking of their moment alone in the bathroom the other day. She wanted him to finish what he'd started but she had been pulled away. She studied him, unsure if he'd live up to the promise he'd made her. It was disappointing. She tried to see everything from his point of view, but it was difficult. Things hadn't been easy for her these past few months. Her life had been turned upside down and she'd followed Jed hoping he'd be something more than a travel companion. There were too many intimate moments.

Shay closed her eyes and remembered the night he'd painted her. The look in his eyes. The feeling of the cool paint spreading across her sensitive skin. She felt her cheeks flush.

"What are you thinking about?" Jed asked. His gaze was intense.

Shay reached across the table to touch him but he pulled his hand away.

"Someone could be watching," Jed said. "Be careful, Shay, Meg and me, we're not a thing."

That hurt, like stones falling into her stomach. She tried not to take it personal. They were playing a part. Shay stood and looked over the landscape. Meg had a great view from her balcony. She could see the Hellion training grounds, the stables, and the forests in the distance.

"I want to go see Nero," Shay said as she turned and headed for the door.

"I can't be caught hanging around you outside the castle. They'll get suspicious."

"Sure." Shay forced a smile to hide her disappointment. "You stay here."

———

Shay made her way down the winding stairs to the first level. Jed trailed behind her, trying to look like he wasn't following her.

The door to the Hellion's lair opened as Shay walked by and Chel stepped out with Klaus close behind.

"Going somewhere?" Chel asked.

"To the stables," Shay said.

"Is this glamour going to last?" Chel asked Jed.

"Of course," Jed replied.

"Remember, you can't go alone," Klaus said.

"Doesn't Meg go places alone?" Shay asked.

"Meg is a bit different. She can hold her own, most of the time," Chel said, motioning for Shay to follow him.

Jed stood in the doorway and watched as the Hellions escorted Shay to the stables.

———

Three new recruit Hellions stood guard at the edge of the courtyard. Osiris, Doyle, and Erebos paced and surveyed the land beyond the castle in the burning caves, standing to attention when the Queen walked by with two senior Hellion guards.

The new recruits stood at attention as she passed.

"Did you smell that?" one asked.

"Yeah. She smelled very familiar."

"That wasn't Meg."

"No, that was someone else."

The new recruits recognized the smell of Shay because they had found her blood trail the night the giant horse-beast broke her leg. They'd found her blood and tasted it and they wanted more.

The younger Hellions moved away, back to their assigned posts so no one would catch them gossiping.

"I want to eat her," one said.

"Slice her arteries and let the blood flow down my throat," another dreamed.

"Fuck." The third one made a fist as his shoulders went rigid. "All this time we searched and she was right under our noses."

Twenty-Two

"Hey." Shay leaned forward and moved her hand to cover Meg's in soothing greeting. Shay knew Meg didn't like to be touched so she let Meg make the final move.

"It's okay." Meg lifted her fist to touch hands. "I'm glad to see you. Are you both doing okay?"

"No complaints from this department," Jed said, inspecting Meg, his fingers tapping on the wooden table in a rapid beat.

"Are you nervous?" Meg asked.

Jed tipped his head toward the Deacon. "You think they know what I am?" He'd never been in the presence of a Deacon before and they were making him feel uneasy.

"I'm sure. They tend to know everything. Or at least they think they do." Meg poured a handful of dirt and rocks under the table.

A few moments later, Skeele walked in the room. Jed stood and clapped him on the shoulder. "Hey man, you alright in there?"

Skeele said, "As well as I can be."

There was a moment of awkwardness.

"I already know," Meg said. "I know he glamoured himself and followed me."

"Hey, man, it worked." Jed smiled and slapped Skeele on the shoulder again. "You brought her back."

Skeele winced and held up a hand. "Easy." He rolled his shoulders. "My assigned method of contrition has been physical."

"They couldn't give you some prayers to say?" Jed asked, lifting his hand, and inspecting Skeele's back. "Dicks."

"I go back next week and they tell me if I'm forgiven." Skeele rubbed his hands together and refused to look in Meg's direction. "My father was a Hellion. I've had worse."

"We have got to get you all out of there," Shay said, patting Meg's hand.

"I have a plan–" Meg started to say.

"It will not work," Skeele argued.

"I've dug a hole. It's almost completed." Meg lowered her voice. "I should be done by next week."

"Good," Skeele said. "At least you can get out of here."

"Wait, wait." Jed held up his hands. "We can't leave Skeele in here." He pressed fingertips to his head for a moment. "Tell me more."

"The hole is small," Meg said. "I can get out. He won't fit." She motioned to Skeele.

Shay turned to face Jed. "She can get out. I can go in. Then you all can storm the place and get Skeele out. Can you still poof from place to place?"

"Not since I was struck by lightning." Meg shook her head.

"Jed could do a glamour. We've been practicing." Shay touched Jed's arm. "Show her. She should know."

Jed's fingers danced in rhythmic spellcasting and Shay turned into a mirror image of Meg.

"Holy shit." Meg leaned forward and touched Shay's hair. "That's amazing."

"Jed's been practicing new spells from his book," Shay said.

"Have you been pretending to be me?" Meg asked.

"We had to," Jed said. "The Deacons showed up and the new Hellions were spreading rumors. She didn't do anything you wouldn't do." A mischievous smile lifted the corners of his mouth. "So next week. You get out. Shay can get in. Skeele, create a distraction. Maybe start a fight.

Then we raid. Watch this." Jed's fingers moved again, and he disappeared then reappeared a few minutes later. "We can get in, get the keys, get Skeele and Shay and get out. You know the layout. You can lead us while we are cloaked."

"Is there a backup plan?" Meg asked.

"We just thought of this like two minutes ago. I haven't thought of a backup plan," Jed said.

Meg nodded. "Let's do it."

———

JED AND SHAY waited at the tree line with Klaus and a handful of Hellions. Meg crawled out of a hole in the ground and ran across the empty field. Klaus grabbed her and pulled her in for a tight hug.

"Ready?" Meg asked Shay.

Shay nodded and began walking toward the hole Meg had crawled out of.

Meg grabbed her arm to stop her. "Just wait for us. We'll get you out."

Shay patted Meg's hand. "I know, Meg. I know you'll get me out."

The little owls hopped around the entrance to the tunnel as Shay climbed inside. The hole was tight and dark. In the distance Shay could see dim light. She focused on the light, crawling as fast as she could.

———

"How long should we give her?" Jed asked.

"A few minutes, then we follow the next Deacon inside," Meg said.

Jed cast his spells turning everyone invisible, then the crew made their way to the front door of the Safe House.

———

"Skeele," the man on the left said. "You ate a family of Newcomers. This is forbidden."

"I was hungry." Skeele replied.

"An entire family, before they had time to reach us." The man at the desk was disgusted. "There are few rules in Hell. Surely you can follow the simplest one."

"It was an emergency." Skeele rolled his shoulders.

"What kind of an emergency?"

"Meg was dying," Skeele said.

"You killed to save the ruler of Hell?"

"Yes." Skeele cleared his throat. "And I'd do it again. I was born and bred to serve the throne."

One man tapped his fingers together. "You are like your father, so faithful to Hell."

"There is no other way to be." Skeele lifted his chin, proud. He was a Hellion.

There is a long pause before the men turned their attention on Shay/Meg.

"We need to discuss your situation," the man to the left said.

Shay pressed her lips together. She glanced at Skeele but couldn't gain a thing from his expression. Shay wished she had notes for this. She had no idea what Meg did on a daily basis besides lose her cool and scare the shit out of everyone. Shay couldn't blame her. The chick was under a lot of pressure.

"The Queen of Hell should not be trying to abort her fetus or be acting recklessly. You were doing drugs to harm your unborn child. God cast you out of the Earthen plane with force. What do you have to say?" the man said.

Shay couldn't say a thing. She couldn't even think of anything to say. She just stood there with her mouth slightly open trying to find words but the only thing going through Shay's mind was what a terrible mess she'd gotten herself into; taking the fall for Meg. Judging from the look on the man's face, this wasn't going to be good. Shay felt like puking. She wished she could rub Meg's face off her own but the glamour wasn't makeup, it didn't work that way. Shay trembled as she stood. She wasn't ready to spend the rest of her life being punished for this. Maybe Jed was right. Maybe she should have gone back to the ranch.

Suddenly a familiar voice broke through the silence, "Break the glamour. This is not her sin to answer for."

Twenty-Three

Nero's eyes flashed open as pure terror sped down the tether he shared with Shay. Something was happening.

Nero was still healing from the Demon wound on his flank and couldn't move. He tried but he could barely lift his head. He could only wiggle his legs. He couldn't even get up on his knees.

Nero had half a mind to kick Jed in the head the next time he saw him. The half-breed man should have protected her. He'd done a good job at in on the Earthen plane, but something was off with the man now that they'd crossed the Veil. Nero could sense it, even from a distance. Jed was uncertain and Nero didn't like it one bit. Someone needed to protect Shay at all times. She couldn't be left to the wild things on this plane.

He hoped Shay would visit soon so he could see her.

He hoped she was okay. Nero hated himself for being injured this badly and unable to roam freely.

The door to the pen opened and a Hellion with curled horns walked in carrying a basket. Nero knew it was time for the basilisk to drain his wound. Usually Shay came during the treatment but she'd been gone for most of the day.

Nero reached across the tether and sensed that the fear had passed. She was now feeling relief and concern. Nero settled his head on the floor of the pen and let the Hellion do his work.

The creature spoke to him like they were brethren. Nero could only think that this Hellion must be too young to realize that horses didn't turn into Crossroads Demons under normal circumstances.

The basilisk treatment didn't hurt. Nero was no longer afraid of the snakelike creature. It was helping him get better. Gone were the days of Nicholas calling the veterinarian to visit Nero on the ranch with antibiotics and steroids. This type of medicine was bizarre, but it worked. Nero sighed, the air blowing out his nose disturbing the hay he was resting on.

Nero saw dried blood on the concrete underneath and remembered injuring Shay. It was an accident. He couldn't remember exactly what happened just that he'd tried to stand and fell onto Shay.

She'd visited since then with a mild limp. Nero didn't know how to apologize. He'd nuzzled her leg and licked her hand and face. He told himself he had to be careful now. He'd changed. He was no longer just a stallion. The ring in his ear itched.

The Hellion removed the basilisk and patted Nero on the flank.

"All done for tonight, chum." The Hellion stood, glancing down at Nero, indifferent. "I hope it's alright that I called you chum."

Nero nodded. He could sense the Hellion feared him. Nero feared himself. He wasn't sure what kind of power he had now, but he could feel it swirling inside of him. There was something dark that hadn't been there before.

He needed to get well so he could help protect Shay. And, before long someone would summon a Crossroads Demon and Nero needed to be ready to step into his new role.

TWENTY-FOUR

The scenery changed quickly for Shay. Thankfully Jed had broken the glamour. Everyone was there and Shay looked like herself again. She moved away from Skeele as Meg took her place, stopping next to Chel as they were all informed that they would be present for Meg's trial. Shay looked to Jed, unsure of what this meant. She didn't want to spend any longer in the Safe House than she had too. It felt wrong and one of the Deacons was staring at her. Sooner or later they were going to find out that she hadn't died and gone to her rightful place. She wasn't a creature of Hell. She was a full blown, pure blood, undead human. And she was quite sure someone in this forsaken building was going to figure that out.

"How do you know Meg?" the Deacon asked Jed.

"I first met her in my shop. She came to me for a tattoo." He held up his arms, showing off his ink.

"Did she know what you were?"

"She didn't know. I had to explain myself."

"You were comfortable explaining yourself to her? You've been in hiding for so long."

"She was in hiding at the time too. We were kindred. Plus, she needed a tattoo, and she could see my blue light." Jed said.

"Any problems after meeting Meg?"

Jed rubbed his neck. "She did bite me once." He laughed lightly. "It didn't hurt. It was kinda nice, kinda sexy." He cleared his throat and sat up straight. "But then she ran off with Sparrow. Our paths crossed again when the zombies started taking over on the Earthen plane."

"And she brought you to Hell against your will?"

"Nope." Jed shook his head with certainty. "Never against my will. She's never forced me to do anything." He paused. "Well, besides tattooing Gabriel but that situation wasn't terrible."

———

Shay took the stand next and the Deacon began his questioning.

"Was that the first time you met Meg?"

"Yes, she rescued us from a house that was under siege with the dead. Jed and I were going to die. Then she showed up at the window and did that *poof* thing. And got us out of there."

"You're full human?" Deacon asked.

"Yes." Shay paused, waiting for something terrible to happen, expecting them to thrust her across the Veil on her ass.

"How do you feel about being in Hell? You don't necessarily belong here."

"I hope to stay here." Shay tilted her head like no one was going to tell her what to do with her life. She didn't want them to know she was scared shitless of these unknown beings. "I spent plenty of time on the Earthen plane and Hell has been much nicer to me. I have freedom and safety here. I have people like I've never had before."

"Does Meg ever scare you?"

"Of course. I can tell she's struggling, but most of us are. I can't imagine the things she feels responsible for. But I can tell you when Nightingale and Sparrow were injured, she did *everything* in her power to get them to safety. And when Thrush was stolen by Demore, she never slept until he was home. Most humans care less about their own children than Meg cared for Thrush. Do you know how many missing children there are on the Earthen plane? How many kids are abused, stolen, left to raise themselves and given nothing?" Shay was shaking. She tucked a piece of blue hair behind her ear. "Meg isn't perfect. Neither am I. But Meg tries, even if she doesn't realize it."

TWENTY-FIVE

THE DEACONS RELEASED Meg after her heart was weighed against the feather of truth. Shay recognized the jar of feathers that Meg had brought back. It was the same jar that sat by her bedside. She recalled being told how Meg lost her first child while she was pregnant. She had been attacked by Hellions. That was before everything. Shay felt for Meg. It was a tragedy no one should have to go through.

Shay was relieved when the scale tipped up, revealing Meg's heart was true. She wasn't evil or bad, just dealing with a boatload of bullshit on a daily basis and trauma that she needed to work through. Then there was the pregnancy. Shay was on edge watching the story unfold in the courtroom. The look on Skeele's face when he realized the child was his, the shame Meg tried to hide, what she'd done to try and get rid of the baby. Shay couldn't judge. The world was a scary place for a pregnant woman. Just look at what happened to Jennifer Asheworth and her two children. Shay glanced at Skeele. He would protect them, she could tell.

Chel flew Shay back to the castle in the burning caves after the trial was over.

Tukka flew Jed.

Jed kept his distance as they got ready for dinner in the ballroom. Nightingale had demanded it.

Jed dressed in his room.

Shay dressed in hers.

Jed was wearing a black silk shirt, black slacks, and cream colored oxfords. He'd tied his hair back in an effort to not look disheveled. He needed a haircut. His hand rested on the door handle of his room. He felt like a dick. He should have been getting ready in the other room with Shay. When they were forced together, he didn't have an issue dropping his guard. Now that there was a second room, he'd gone cold and wasn't sure why. He promised he wouldn't do this. He'd pressed her against the wall that night and promised he'd never do it again. He was going to have to fix this and get his head straight. This was the last night he could live like this. He couldn't live in fear his entire life.

Jed stepped into the living room of the suite and

waited for Shay. He was trying to think of what to say to her, but then she stepped out of the bedroom.

Her blowtorch blue hair was arranged in a half updo with curls hanging against her neck. She was wearing a gauzy blue dress that accentuated every curve. She looked like a goddess.

Suddenly, Jed couldn't form words. She had so much skin showing. He swallowed hard.

"Ready?" Shay asked with the rise of her brows.

"Yeah." He followed her. He stumbled to get to the door before she did and held it open.

"You look nice," Shay said. "Did you find that or did it just appear in the closet?"

"It was there." Jed's mouth felt full of cotton as he struggled to find words. He was too busy looking at her.

"This too," Shay said as she smoothed a hand over her dress. She didn't tell Jed that the heels made her leg ache and she did her best not to limp.

Chel and Klaus were in the hallway, lingering. Both were dressed nicely in black slacks and silky button-downs.

"Come on, clowns," Klaus prodded. "We are going to be late.

———

Chel lingered too close to Shay. He smiled a lot and told Shay jokes that she didn't quite understand because she hadn't lived in Hell her whole life. Chel had to explain most of them, but Shay laughed and her gaze met Jed's as he stood near the window and sipped from a glass of wine.

Jed was annoyed; Chel was fucking with him and would continue to do so. He knew it.

Meg and Skeele were on the balcony, then the air. Everyone saw her drop from the sky and ran to watch.

Shay gripped the stone balcony railing and leaned forward. Chel pulled her back. Jed glared, ready to push Chel off.

Suddenly, Shay turned, smiling. "Did you see it?" she asked, moving closer to Jed. She looked so pretty in the blue dress. Jed wished they were elsewhere, alone.

He shook his head. "I didn't see."

"Meg got her wings. They are beautiful. Kinda gray. Is that because she's half Angel and half Demon?"

"Probably," Jed replied, taking another sip of his wine, trying to drink off the edginess that was growing with each minute.

"Will you get wings?" Shay asked, touching his shoulder.

"Nope." Jed shook his head. "My kind doesn't have wings." He paused. "Well, some are born with them but they're usually too small and then they all die anyway. So..."

"Jeeze," Shay said. "That's freaking depressing."

"I know." It was a shit set up. With wings and magic, he could have stood a better chance with all the creatures he'd battled on the Earthen plane. He could have saved his mother that night on the train.

The song changed and Shay turned to see Noah at the record player, turning up the volume. *Billie Jean* played and nearly everyone began dancing to the beat.

"Want to dance?" Shay asked as she moved toward the dance floor.

Jed downed the last of his wine and turned to set the glass down. When he turned again, Chel was dancing with Shay. She laughed, touching his shoulder. Chel's hand was on her hip, his large frame bent over her, whispering in her ear.

It was Jed's fault and he knew it. He had gone hot then cold. He shouldn't have. His worst fear was seeing Shay hurt or worse, dead. He couldn't keep her at arm's length. Living in peace was all he'd ever wanted, and that's finally what they had here. Until Chel came along.

Rage flooded Jed. Absolute, unadulterated rage like never before in his life. He was going to kill the Hellion in front of everyone. Right. Now.

Jed marched across the ballroom to where everyone

was dancing, his fingertips tingling with magic. Sparks flew from him only to sizzle on the tile floor. He cracked his knuckles as he got closer, ready to send Chel to another plane. Preferably the Ether from where he'd never return.

Just as Michael Jackson hit the high note in *Billie Jean*, Jed flung a shot of electricity with the flip of his wrist. It was barely battle magic but it was enough to send Chel flying across the room on his ass.

Shay's eyes were big as she turned to face Jed.

Jed stepped closer, grabbed her hand and twirled her until she slammed against his chest.

The music came to a static and abrupt stop. Noah was changing songs. *Pretty Young Thing* blasted through the speakers.

Jed shot a glance of thanks to Noah. He wasn't a skilled dancer but he could keep up with Michael Jackson's beat in this song.

Jed turned them both so his back was to the crowd, he pressed his mouth against Shay's ear. "Mine," he growled before turning her quickly, holding her at arm's length just for a second before tugging her back to his chest. He fit his leg between her thighs and took her hand, guiding it up his chest and around his neck.

His large hand stretched across her back and pulled her tight against him so every part of their bodies that could touch, did.

Jed knew the Hellions were nothing but animals half the time. Their sense of smell was strong and he couldn't forget that had Chel shamed him for not making Shay smell like him. He'd rub himself all over her to keep them away starting right now. Jed guided her, grinding together with the beat of the song. He wished there was no clothing between them.

Shay's lips were open, her tongue darted out to wet her lips as she watched him with half-lidded eyes.

Jed's free hand cupped her cheek, slid into her hair, and tilted her head back. He searched her eyes for fear. She wasn't afraid. She rarely ever was. She was human but she was strong. He knew it. He wished he'd been conscious that night she killed the Angel on the Earthen plane. He was sure she looked spectacular, just like she did tonight.

Jed's mouth closed over Shay's. He kissed her deeply, for all to see.

The room erupted in clapping.

"It's about fuckin' time!" Noah shouted.

Twenty-Six

Alastor followed the black sludge footprints and they led him straight to Lucifer's castle. He knelt near a cluster of trees. In the ochre cast of Hellsky night, he noticed a dried puddle of blackness. Alastor moved to the middle of the crumbling road and touched his finger to the dried inky fluid and sniffed it. He closed his eyes. There it was. Sugar and sunshine, pure. He could smell the hint of her in the fluid on his finger. He sniffed the air. The Crossroads Demon was here. And so was Shay.

It had been decades since Alastor was last at the castle. He didn't see any Hellion patrols as he moved closer. He could hear music and laughter.

Wingbeats overhead startled him. Alastor shifted back into the shadows and sank to the ground, watching the shadows that passed overhead.

It was a Hellion and... the Queen. Last he'd heard she couldn't fly. It appeared things had changed. Alastor cursed this transformation. He'd hoped someone would battle Meg for the throne and things could go back to the way they were when Lucifer ruled. He doubted Meg would let him continue with the skin trades if she ever found out. She'd shut it down. She'd brought too much light to Hell.

He waited, crouched and planning while the two flew overhead, letting out a breath of irritation when they finally returned to the castle. He studied the grounds, the patrols, he'd wait here for as long as he needed to and find his way in.

Twenty-Seven

Shay woke with a startle. She was dripping in sweat and naked. Jed stirred and Shay watched the sheet slip down revealing the sharp curve of his back.

A twinge in her chest forced her to look out the window. Shay grabbed Jed's silk button-down and put it on as she walked to the balcony. The twinge tightened and Shay rubbed her sternum. In the distance, she could see lights on in the stables. Then, the unmistakable panicked neighing of Nero.

"Nero!" Shay whispered.

Shay ran into the room and found her jeans and boots. She buttoned Jed's shirt as she grabbed her gun from the closet and her hunting knife. Then she ran out of the bedroom.

She ran down the stairwell two at a time, ran down the

hallway and shoved the door to the courtyard open with her shoulder and a grunt.

"Nero!" Shay shouted as she ran across pebbled walkways. It was dark, nearly pitch black. Shay's eyes were adjusting to the night. The only light came from the barn in the distance.

Nero whinnied again.

Shay ran faster, tripping over rocks and uneven terrain. She had made it off the walkway and was making a beeline toward the stables.

She made it to the barn and shoved open the door. The lights blinded her and Shay held a hand up to shield her eyes.

"Told you she'd come," Osiris said.

"Like a fly to honey." Doyle gripped his blade.

"What's with her and this horse?" Erebos jerked hard on the harness tied to Nero.

Nero reared up, or at least tried to. He was still weak from the healing wound on his flank. He limped twice then slid to the ground.

"I'm going to kill it," Doyle said as he moved closer to Nero, blade gleaming.

"No!" Shay said. She was aiming her gun in Doyle's direction. "Don't you dare touch that horse."

The three Hellions laughed. Shay had never seen them before. Unease filled her gut. This was not good but she'd be damned if she wasn't going to stand her ground and protect her best friend since childhood. She wasn't a coward even though the tiny voice in her head was screaming at her to run.

Erebos moved faster than Shay had ever seen anyone move. He punched her wrist and the handgun went flying.

Shay scanned the dimly lit stable as she dropped to the ground and rolled away from Erebos's grip. Her wrist and leg ached as she scrambled to her feet toward the dropped gun. Doyle kicked the gun to a dark corner, straddled her back and grabbed a fistful of blue hair.

Shay winced as he pulled her up to her knees.

Doyle sniffed her neck. "Oh yes. We've tasted your blood before." His long tongue licked her skin.

Shay struggled and gained just enough distance to draw back her arm and punch Doyle in the knee. He let go of her hair. Shay dropped to the ground, rolled to her back, and faced the Hellion straddling her. Her wrist ached but she had one shot to get away from this bastard. With everything she had, she punched him right in the balls.

Doyle roared in pain and dropped to the ground.

Erebos and Osiris roared in laughter.

"You let that tiny human touch your balls," Erebos said, smiling, revealing sharp teeth. "She'll be touching mine next."

"I'm not touching any of you." Shay lunged for her

gun in the dark corner, landing on her stomach and sliding across the hay. She clambered, her fingers feeling the slick metal of the gun. She grabbed it.

Osiris grabbed onto both of Shay's ankles and dragged her back.

Shay rolled, aimed, and shot him in the shoulder.

"Bitch," Osiris sneered as blood leaked from his shoulder and soaked his uniform.

Shay shot him again and he let go of her ankles.

A dark shadow was coming for her. Fearing another fist to the wrist, she rolled, twisted, and braced her back against the wall of the stables.

Erebos was coming at her. She shot him twice, hitting him in the gut and grazing his neck. He came at her faster, grabbing her by the neck and shoulder and dragging her up the wall.

Shay's feet scraped the floor to support her body so her neck didn't snap. He pressed his arm to her neck, securing her with one arm. He tore at the loose shirt, ripping the buttons to reveal her shoulder.

Erebos made a nauseating sound as he licked his lips and leaned in, eager to consume her.

Shay used her last bullet to shoot Erebos in the foot. It bounced off his boot and clanked against the concrete floor. She rotated the gun in her hand, holding the scalding hot barrel, ready to hit him in the head with the heavy handle.

"No," Erebos said as he pressed his arm against her neck until she couldn't breathe.

Shay's head swam. Her vision blurred. She didn't want to die like this.

She barely heard the groan of breaking wood as Chel ripped the stable door off its hinges and tossed it aside. Skeele and Tukka were close behind.

Lightning crackled and arcane wisps of smoke slithered along the floor as Jed entered the barn.

Erebos was holding Shay up against the stall wall with an arm pressed across her neck. He'd bitten her shoulder and blood coated his lips. Doyle and Osiris were close, anticipating their turn.

"Make her stop bleeding," Skeele demanded of Jed.

Osiris was licking a cut on Shay's arm. Doyle was feeding from a wound on her leg.

The small space erupted in chaos.

The commanding Hellions knew this would be a challenge. With fresh blood in their systems, the new recruits would be just as feral as a Demon from the forests.

Nero got up but was struggling to stay on his feet.

Jed's finger's twitched as he drew on power from deep in his bones. Ropes of shadows wrapped around Erebos and tore him away from Shay.

The younger Hellion hissed. He reached out at the last

second and grabbed Shay by her shirt, dragging her along as Jed flung Erebos across the room.

Nero was watching and judging the right time to kick Erebos in the head. He didn't anticipate Erebos dragging Shay and when Nero kicked, his hoof glanced off Shay's right thigh, hitting Erebos in the stomach with the sharp hoof tearing skin open.

Erebos dropped Shay and gripped his stomach wound.

Jed sent a string of power toward Erebos, closing the distance between them. He slammed Erebos through the wall of the stables, leaving a gaping hole to the outdoors. He collected Osiris and Doyle with black wisps of smoke wrapped around their necks until they went unconscious. He laid the three Hellions in the grass outside the stables.

They were in direct sight of the Hellion new recruit barracks. Recruits were gathered around the windows and doors, watching.

"Should we take them to the dungeon?" Tukka suggested.

"No." Skeele was pacing beside the unconscious recruits. "The others need to see this."

Skeele gripped their heads, one by one, and twisted with quick movement, effectively snapping their necks.

———

JED TURNED, searching for Shay. Chel had her in his arms, bleeding, bone sticking through the skin on her right leg. Again.

Chel set Shay on the ground in front of Jed. "Fix her. Now. We must get her to safety."

Jed dropped to his knees. He splayed his hands. Whispered words that sounded like a good promise. Like a sunset over the lake. Like a humming prayer. He'd whispered them not too long ago as Shay lay in the infirmary. He didn't have Teari this time but Jed knew what to do. White light streamed from his hands and mended blood vessels to stop the bleeding. He paused over the exposed bone. Teari had healed that last time, and Shay had been unconscious. He barely tapped the bone with a tendril of light.

Shay screamed in agony.

Chel dropped to his knees opposite Jed. He pulled off his belt and wound the ends in his fists. "Open your mouth," he said to Shay. "Bite down."

Shay bit the leather between her teeth. Chel leaned close to her face, did his best to ignore the smell of fresh blood. He had more control than most and he remained in control as memories of Yelena played in his mind. He wouldn't allow Shay to suffer the same fate of premature death.

"This is gonna hurt like a sonofabitch," Chel warned Shay. "But you can do it."

Shay nodded, blue hair matted to her face by blood and tears and sweat.

Chel turned to Jed and nodded. "Do it."

Jed's expression was tortured as he met Shay's eyes. "I'm sorry," he said before turning back to her broken leg. He whispered words that sounded like a good promise. Like a sunset over the lake. Like a humming prayer. Again. And again. And again. White tendrils dove into her leg and reset the bone. Her femur settled back into place. Jed did his best to ignore the sounds of Shay screaming against the belt between her teeth.

Skeele was watching the lights go out in the new recruit barracks with Klaus. Their large bodies shielded Shay and Jed from any onlookers.

Jed chanted. He mended the bone, the ligaments, the torn muscle. He worried that she'd need a blood transfusion but decided against it since she was still awake and there was significantly less blood than before. He continued his work fixing her leg, then the soft skin of her shoulder. He made sure the bite mark was completely healed. She would carry no scarring of a Hellion's teeth on her neck. He could at least give her that. The scar on her leg would be another issue.

Jed was glowing like a torch with the amount of magic

he was using. There was no way the Hellions could shield it. He was sure the Seven Kingdoms of Heaven could see him all the way down in Hell right now. His light blasting between planes.

When he finally stopped, Shay's eyes were closed.

"Done?" Chel asked.

Jed nodded, his voice hoarse, throat dry and burning. His glowing aura dimmed as his shoulders sagged.

Shay's eyes fluttered open groggily.

Chel removed his belt from between her teeth and began putting it on again.

"He has to go," Chel warned. "Twice now he's broken your leg." Chel was shaking his head. "We can't keep him here."

"No!" Shay cried. "Don't send him away. It wasn't his fault." She'd lost everything and she so desperately wanted to hold onto Nero.

"We have to go back. Now." Skeele was checking on Nero. The giant horse was unconscious again.

Jed was lifting Shay off the ground as she reached toward the barn. "The wall is missing," she said.

"He's not going anywhere," Chel said. "For now."

Skeele motioned for them to move. Jed held Shay close.

"I can walk," Shay said.

"Barely." Jed refused to look at her as he kept pace with

the Hellions, headed toward the courtyard and door to the castle.

Rocks crunched under Jed's boots as he stepped up.

"What was that?" Chel asked.

The group paused and turned, everyone watched the darkness.

Skeele turned slowly. A gentle wind blew across the courtyard. He held up a hand. Chel and Tukka turned to stone, awaiting orders.

"Something else is here," Skeele said.

The Hellions lurked, pantherlike in their movements as they surveyed the courtyard but didn't stray far from Shay and Jed.

"Get inside," Skeele commanded. Skeele took to the sky, blade in hand.

Chel hurried Jed to move faster until they were behind the door to the castle.

"Get to your rooms, half-breed," Chel demanded. "Now."

TWENTY-EIGHT

JED KICKED the door to their suite closed. "Fucking Christ," he muttered as he checked the wards. "This was a bad idea." He pulled a piece of charcoal from his pocket and drew a large rune on the back of the door, whispered a spell that sounded like fate and death dancing. Then he took the etched blade and cut two of his fingertips, drawing on the door in his own blood.

"What's going on?" Shay winced and held onto a nearby chair for support. She'd never seen him use blood in his runes and the gravity of the situation worried her.

Jed approached her, livid, magic burning in his fingertips. "Don't you ever leave while I'm sleeping again. I'll ward every room so you can't. I want you to have your freedom but you have to have some sense of danger here.

We are in Hell. There are Demons everywhere. You are human. It was past midnight and black as pitch outside."

"Nero was in trouble!" Shay argued.

"Nero is a Demon now. He can take care of himself. He's no longer a foal on the prairie."

Shay was shaking her head. "No. He's mine. He's my horse. He's not a Demon, he's good and gentle–"

"He broke your leg. Twice."

"He didn't mean it. Those Hellions are at fault. Not him. Not Nero." Tears burned Shay's eyes. "Accidents happen."

"Accidents like you slipping out in the night and getting into trouble? Life or death kind of trouble?" Jed's hands wrapped around her wrists and tugged her close. "I'm tempted to lock you in this room forever." He searched her face for understanding. "I'll hold you down and tattoo runes all over your body, every inch of you. You cannot ever do this again. I will not lose you." He kissed her, hard and punishing. Everything he'd feared had almost come true tonight. The moment he let his guard down and opened his heart, he nearly lost everything he cared about. Her.

Shay winced.

"Show me where it hurts," Jed demanded.

"I'm fine."

"You're not." Jed took her arm, extending it and searching her skin for injuries.

"You've used enough magic on me tonight."

"Tell me."

She pointed to a bruise on her jaw. Warmth flowed from his fingertips as he found every scratch and bruise on Shay's skin. He healed them, then pressed open-mouthed kisses to her heated skin, peeling her clothes away as he worked. He stopped at the scar on her thigh, worried that her femur would never be completely the same if she broke it again. He had noticed when she tried to hide her limp. He pressed his fingertips against the scar and whispered words that sounded like a cracking fire on a cold night. The scar remained. He pressed his lips against her thigh and hoped it would heal completely. He wouldn't pray. He knew better than to do that.

Jed's hands slid up her body possessively. "Now, I'm gonna check you for zombie bites." He kissed her shoulder, exposed by his torn and too big shirt she was wearing.

Shay sucked in a breath. "I didn't get bit."

"How can you be so sure?" Jed asked with a wicked smile. "I'm just going to double check."

"What about the others?" Shay asked as Jed lifted her and carried her to the bedroom.

"They definitely aren't invited."

"Skeele said *something* was here," Shay clarified, worry in her voice.

"Sounds like a *them* problem."

Jed kicked the bedroom door closed.

Twenty-Nine

Nero's eyes flashed open. He smelled blood and it wasn't his. Self-loathing flooded his body as he took in the scene before him. He lifted his head. The stable was destroyed. Blood was everywhere. It wasn't just Shay's.

Nero heard a noise and looked toward the gaping hole in the wall. Noah was standing there with the basket.

"What a shit show," Noah said as he walked past the dead bodies.

Nero whinnied in agreement.

"Best you just stay down, beast." Noah kneeled and pulled the basilisk out of the basket. He glared at Nero. "I'm not sure if you remember what happened here."

Nero stared.

"Seems there was a fight. From what I was told you managed to kick Shay's leg and break it. Again."

Nero neighed sadly. He wasn't aiming for her but his reactions were slow with the poison that was running through his system.

Noah held the basilisk as it attached to the wound on Nero's flank.

"I don't think they're going to let you stay here." Noah shook his head.

Nero looked away.

"We'll leave this on for longer. Just in case they make you leave in the morning."

Nero nodded, wishing he could speak in plain language. He sensed there was something different about Noah. He was also tethered to someone. Surely the ghost would understand if he could tell him that Shay and he were tethered also. Nero could never stay away for long. He had to see her. Had to be there for her. It was his duty. He could never repay Shay for saving his life.

Nero's side twitched as the basilisk drew deeply from the wound. Nero felt the poison within his body being drawn out.

"Is it getting better?" Noah asked.

Nero nodded.

"Guess Teari's timing was off. I'll tell her ten minutes isn't enough for Demon poison." Noah shifted and glanced at the mess surrounding them.

Silence stretched between them. Nero felt his body

growing stronger. The weakness and ache that had rampaged his body was lifting. He held still and waited for the basilisk to continue.

Nero's legs ached from days of unuse. That familiar itch to run was intensifying in his body. Nero hadn't realized how much this illness had taken from him. He hadn't run in the mountains in ages. Something wild was slithering under his skin, waiting to be released.

Noah packed up the basilisk and stood. He filled the water basin for Nero.

"Well, giant horse," Noah said. "That boo boo looks like nothing but a scratch now. It's been a pleasure to serve you. All this ranks up there on the list of crazy shit I've experienced since arriving in Hell. Never gets old. Does it?"

Nero whinnied and lowered his head, nudging Noah's hand.

"I guess this is a thank you?" Noah took the hint and stroked Nero's nose. "You don't seem that bad. It's no surprise Shay loves you so much."

Noah returned to the castle and left Nero amid the destroyed barn. Nero felt better than he had in ages. His leg no longer ached and the burning pain was gone from his flank. He was suddenly starving. Nero walked to the grain bin and helped himself.

The angst slithering under his skin grew stronger.

Nero shivered and stretched his neck. He drank nearly all the water Noah had filled the basin with. It didn't quench his thirst.

Nero snapped his teeth together in gnarled chatter. Something strange was happening to his body. He left the stables through the giant hole in the wall and noticed the three bodies on the ground. Their necks had been snapped. Nero recognized them as the Hellions that had attacked Shay.

Nero didn't know much about Hell and the creature he had become. There was no warning. No book. No horse educational video. He didn't know that the Demon poison had prevented him from changing into his new form. He was more than night lightning or a black hole, he was more than a friend of a human girl, he was more than just a Crossroads Demon. He'd survived the poison, he'd jumped through the Veil. He had goodness in his heart no matter how black the blood pumping through his veins had turned. That didn't stop him from turning into a monster.

Nero changed forms. It only happened for a split second, under the ochre glow of Hellsky moon. He shivered, gnashed his teeth together, tensed his body, and *changed*. Nero was already huge but in that second he doubled in size, his long black tail and mane became stiff as needles and sharp as razorblades. His veins became giant ropes of obsidian, twining and swirling under his skin like protective armor. The hunger was the worst part. The oats did nothing to fill his stomach.

The three bodies of the dead Hellions were right there. And Nero ate them.

-The End-

Preview: Midnight Serenade (Veil of Shadows 10) [Unedited]

About Midnight Serenade

Trapped between Heaven and Hell, Jed faces his demons while Shay's fate hangs in the balance.

Jed finds himself ensnared in a perilous web of darkness and despair as he confronts his inner demons. Shay's fate teeters on the edge of oblivion, her very existence hanging in the balance.

Meanwhile, amidst the chaos of the infernal realm, Alastor, driven by a thirst for vengeance, searches for a means to infiltrate the castle and unleash his wrath upon those who have wronged him. But his path is fraught with danger, and the shadows of betrayal lurk around every corner.

As if the looming threat of Alastor's vengeance weren't enough, Nero's transformation into a monstrous entity sends shockwaves through the kingdom, casting a pall of fear and uncertainty over all who dwell within its walls. Outside the castle, a malevolent presence lurks, waiting to unleash its fury upon any who dare to cross its path.

In this dark and twisted tale of betrayal, redemption, and the struggle for survival, Jed and Shay must navigate a treacherous landscape where the line between friend and foe blurs and the consequences of their choices echo through the halls of Hell itself. Will they find the strength to overcome the darkness that threatens to consume them, or will they be lost to its unforgiving embrace?

Chapter 1

Alastor heard an echo that sounded more like the crunching of bones than the breaking of sticks underfoot. He shifted on his haunches and watched the Hellions survey the perimeter of the castle grounds.

Alastor gripped the basilisk tooth knife in his fist and turned only to find... nothing. There was nothing there.

The hairs rising on the back of his neck told him otherwise. Something wasn't right here. Alastor began backing away. He needed a better plan. He couldn't barrel on in—someone was walking nearby. It was a Hellion. Alastor got a good look at him. This Hellion was clearly young and pushed through the ranks to go on guard duty. This was a rookie move for the Queen's Commander to allow. A Hellion recruit on guard duty wouldn't expect a Demon like Alastor to be hiding in the forest, searching for a way in.

Alastor waited until the Hellion got closer, and closer, and closer.

The Hellion was barely past puberty. Too bad. Alastor had to take this moment. He stood quickly and shoved the basilisk knife into the soft flesh under the Hellion's jaw. The Hellion never made a sound, simply died in the forest.

Alastor made quick work of getting the Hellion's uniform off. Then he stripped and put on the uniform. He took the blade, knowing it wouldn't work for him. It was common knowledge that a Hellion's blade was enchanted to only cut for its owner. He had to look the part.

Alastor shivered. His bloodlines didn't run into Hellion territory. He knew nothing about honor and duty. Alastor was a different kind of Demon. His bloodline went to the root. Alastor could never join the Hellion ranks, but he could pretend. He could pretend until he made his way into that castle, killed the half-breed Angel and took what was his. *Shay*. Alastor would use her as he wished, then sell her, piece by piece, until he'd collected all the money and power that was lost when his skin trade was disrupted.

Chapter 2

Jed was used to warding doors so no one could enter his room. He wasn't used to the opposite side of the door being locked so he couldn't exit. He tried the handle again and pulled. It wouldn't budge.

Jed's fingertips tingled as he drew on magic to open the door. He tried unlocking spells, opening spells, transparency spells but nothing worked. He paced the suite until he finally stopped next to the bed. Shay was sleeping. She'd been sleeping for more than a day. It had been a rough night with her breaking her leg again. She'd lost a lot of blood. He was sure that she was beyond tired after everything.

Jed bent and touched her forehead, remembering that he'd kept her up longer than he should have that night. Jed couldn't help it. He'd almost lost her. Need built within him as he remembered how he'd bathed the blood off her body, then carried her to the bed and gave her a few good reasons to never sneak off in the night again. There wasn't an inch of her body that he hadn't explored with his mouth, his tongue, his fingers. Desire stirred. He wanted her again. Again and again. Forever.

Shay shifted, rolling onto her stomach, and pulling her right leg up. She was naked. The scar along her thigh was all he could see.

Jed lowered himself to the floor and kneeled. He moved his hand over the mark. There was something different about it. He closed his eyes and tried to get a sense of what was going on with the scar. His fingers glowed as he inspected the edges of it. He'd healed her femur, repaired the bone, muscle and blood vessels. Something wasn't quite right though. The healing magic took, but it was almost as though something was lingering under her skin. Dirt, or a shard of... something. Jed wasn't sure. He wasn't a healer, simply could use his magic to heal. Maybe he should consult Teari? The only problem was, he couldn't leave the room.

The sun was rising. Maybe Chel had locked them in here because whatever had spooked Skeele was still lurking in the forests surrounding the castle. Locking them up was a bit overboard. Certainly, they'd be safe within the walls of the castle. They'd be warm at least. The winter chill was worsening.

Jed glanced at Shay's face. Chel probably didn't trust Shay to follow directions. Nero was still on the premises, roaming. He'd stood under the window and neighed sadly, calling for Shay. It was strange that the horse knew exactly which window hers was.

Shay sighed in her sleep. The sheet fell, revealing her bare shoulder. Her hair was longer, down the middle of her back. It had grown from one of the many healing spells he'd used.

Jed rubbed his face. He had plenty of questions, but right now, no one wanted anything from either of them. He stripped off his clothes and crawled into bed next to Shay. She didn't protest as he dragged her body close to his and wrapped himself around her.

He could stay like this forever with her. Warm, safe, trapped. He'd let his guard down. It was easy, not looking over a shoulder and expecting danger every moment.

Jed pulled Shay's hair aside, revealing her neck. He watched her pulse, inspected her healed skin from the Hellion bite. He pressed his lips there, then across her neck to the sensitive skin behind her ear.

Shay nudged him with her hips. It was barely a movement, but he felt it and took it as an invitation. His free hand drifted down her body, lazing toying with her skin, her breasts, the plane of her stomach, edge of her ribs, the swell of her hips. Shay moaned and pressed against him. He parted her legs and nudged inside of her. He kissed her neck, her shoulder, and when his hand pressed against her lower belly, edging him deeper, her hand wrapped around his wrist and they fell away together.

Chapter 3

Nero nibbled at the sweet grass that grew along the tree line. A crew was fixing the damaged barn but Nero had no desire to be contained by four walls ever again. He considered drinking from the nearby ponds but the Hellion who'd called him chum left out buckets of water. Nero was glad he wouldn't have to risk a stomach ache.

Nero stood near the Hellion training grounds, watching them train in combat. Something was wrong with Shay. Nero could sense her fatigue. After that night in the barn, the tether connecting them felt stronger, tighter. He wasn't sure why.

When she didn't come to the window, he'd felt disparaged. All he wanted was to see her and make sure she was okay. He'd apologize if he could. He never meant to hurt her. Never in his life would he do that intentionally. She was small and fragile, and he was so much bigger than he used to be. Still, Nero would watch over Shay. Nero would help her like she'd helped him in when he was a foal.

He felt much stronger now that the basilisk had removed all the poison from his wound. There was barely an ache as it finished healing overnight.

The Hellion named Chel had threatened to make him leave, but there had been no official order. Nero liked the castle grounds. It was warmer than the forests and the mountains. He'd found a crack in an outcropping of rocks that leaked warm steam. Nero never wanted to return to that hovel. He'd do everything to stay here, close to Shay. This wasn't the Earthen plane. There were too many dangers.

"It's still out there," Klaus said to Tukka. "Whatever Skeele sensed is still here, somewhere."

Nero was listening and wandered closer.

"Keep up the reconnaissance." Tukka crossed his arms and frowned. "We're down three Hellions. We need to replace them."

"Call upon the families for more recruits. They'll be young." Klaus motioned to the recruits, and they switched sparring partners.

Nero nudged Klaus's shoulder, wishing he could speak and tell them he'd help.

"What do you want, beast?" Klaus smiled as he stroked Nero's nose. "You probably don't need to be pet like a puppy."

Nero huffed and nudged him again. He didn't mind the contact, it made him remember the days when everyone pet him. He'd received much less affection since Hell became his home.

"What about the family out there at the chapel," Tukka motioned to the road. "Whatever's out there could be hunting them."

"Let's hope not." Klaus rubbed his white beard. "If anything happens to that baby, Meg will lose it."

Nero's ears twitched. He didn't realize there was a child so close. Since he had nothing to do, he decided he'd go investigate. Shay needed him but he could help protect the child as well. It was the least he could do for moving in uninvited.

Nero walked away from the Hellions and made his way across the yard. He left hoofprints on the rock path and overgrown grass. Nero avoided the stained dirt where the three Hellions had died. He didn't want to remember that night, what he'd done, or what he'd turned into.

Nero shook his head before glancing up at Shay's window. It was still closed, the curtains pulled. He hoped she'd come out soon.

He passed the courtyard with the dead-looking tree

in the center and headed for the main road that led to the graveyard. He'd seen it the night he ran here to find Shay.

Nero took his time, taking in his surroundings, searching for whatever threat was out here. His pace was lazy and slow but he made it to the graveyard faster than he expected.

There was a fence surrounding the chapel and Nero could hear the laughter of a young child. He remembered the joy of seeing children in Lame Deer and wandered closer.

The fence was tall but Nero could still see over it. He was sure he could leap over it if he needed to.

"Oh look, Thrush," a familiar voice said. "It's Nero."

He recognized Noah.

"Horsey," Noah said to the chubby baby in his arms. "Want to pet the horsey?"

"Are you sure that's a horse?" a woman's voice asked.

Nero tilted his head to see a woman with dark hair walking closer. Ah, Nightingale. He remembered now. The mother to the baby. Noah spoke of her when he'd visited Nero for the basilisk therapy.

"Big horsey," Noah said, bouncing the baby in his arms. He stopped near the fence. "How'd you get that tall, Nero? Just a few days ago you were shorter."

Nero huffed and shook his head. He wasn't sure how

tall he was, just that he could see over this fence and he was sure he'd never been able to do that before.

"Suppose you can't really tell me." Noah lifted baby Thrush and held him closer. "Horsey. Touch him."

A fat little hand reached out and touched the side of Nero's face. The baby laughed and babbled.

"Does he want a treat?" Nightingale asked, passing a carrot into Thrush's hand, and helping him hold it up.

Nero took the carrot—easy and careful like Shay trained him—and chewed it. Watching Thrush giggle as he crunched loudly.

Nightingale looked up as a shadow passed overhead. A Hellion was flying, scoping out the grounds. Nero wished he could speak and tell them that something dangerous was in the forest. He watched Nightingale closely and got the sense that whatever it was, should be afraid of her.

The wind was chilly, and baby Thrush was bundled up in a snowsuit. His cheeks red.

Nightingale rubbed her arms and shivered. "We should get him inside," she said. "It's going to snow tonight."

Noah held Thrush close. "You stay warm tonight, Nero. Visit us again whenever you'd like."

Nero whinnied before turning and wandering toward the road.

As he walked, he heard Nightingale's voice mention *giant* and *Demon horse* and *dangerous*. But, the good thing about being a horse was he didn't have to give two shits about what people said about him.

Snowflakes were falling, leaving stark white dots against Nero's coat. He shook his head as they collected on his eyelashes.

A strange smell wafted from the forest. Nero paused and moved closer. Frozen leaves crunched under his hooves as he searched for the smell. It was familiar, something rotting. He wondered if this was what the Hellions were worried about. He searched and searched. Tree trunks scraped against his sides as he walked through the forest. Some trees bent or snapped off, too close together to accommodate his size.

Finally, he found it. A rotting corpse of a Demon under the leaves. A sense of pride filled Nero. He'd solved their problem. Found the smell and the creature the Hellions were wary of. There was no danger after all.

Nero returned to the castle grounds and approached the first Hellion he came across.

He neighed and nodded his head. Walked back and forth, tugged on the Hellion's uniform with his teeth.

"Get away," the Hellion said, stepping back. "Shoo." He gripped his blade.

Nero gave up. This creature wasn't understanding that he had to show him something. He left and went in search of someone who might listen to him. Maybe that Hellion who'd called him chum, or their leader Skeele, or maybe he'd go back and get Noah. Who he really needed was Shay, she'd understand that he was trying to tell them something important.

CHAPTER 4

Then

Chel lay in the Hellion recruit barracks, hands behind his head, feet crossed, waiting for the bullshit to start. He'd been awake for hours, waiting for the Commander to come in shouting and dragging him and the rest of the Hellion recruits out of bed. His father had warned him it would be like this. His family was bred to be Hellions but something changed when Lucifer died and the new Queen took over. There was a shift in the edge that drove Hellions to violence. They held back, anticipated, contained their rage for only necessary times. They slept lighter and trained harder. New concepts had been taught like compassion and delayed reaction. In two days Chel would be released on forty-eight hours of leave. He had nowhere else to go besides home.

Chel would never forget when he stepped through the

threshold of his childhood home, the familiar sights and sounds of his childhood greeted him with a bittersweet embrace. The air was still heavy with grief, the weight of loss palpable in every corner, especially the kitchen where his mother spent most of her time.

Chel's mother hadn't spoken much during dinner, her eyes hollow with sorrow, she sat in silence, hands clasped tightly in her lap as if trying to hold onto the fragments of her shattered world. She'd been like this since Yelena went missing.

His father was a brooding figure in his favorite lounge chair, radiating an aura of simmering anger, his jaw clenched with unspoken fury. Chel remembered the same Demon from childhood. He hadn't changed a bit.

"Utter bullshit," his father slammed a fork down. "I didn't send my only son off to be a pussy in the ranks." He reached across the table and grabbed Chel by the collar of his uniform. "You listen to me, you smile and nod but deep down understand that mentality will not save a soul. You need to be quick, exact. You need to kill. That is a Hellion's duty."

"Yes, sir," Chel had nodded and stared into his father's red eyes until the moment of rage passed.

There it was. Sparrow, the Hellion Commander, had mentioned the rage that drove previous ages. They were going to be different, better. Sparrow's teaching and guidance was always inspiring, but Chel didn't tell his father that. He finished his dinner and came to the realization that this might be the last time he visited his parents.

Chel's mother stood and began clearing dishes. She left the dusty plate at the setting next to Chel. Yelena's seat. She'd never cleared the place setting after all these years. It was like she was expecting Yelena to come running back home, burst through the door for dinner. She never came, she would never come. Yelena had been gone for years. Kidnapped and murdered by wrath-filled Demons.

Chel's gaze shifted to the empty space where Yelena once sat, a void that echoed with the haunting absence of her presence. The ache of her loss weighed heavily on his heart, a reminder of the fragility of life and the cruel whims of fate.

As the evening wore on, Chel found himself grappling with a revelation that gnawed at the core of his being. His father's violent outbursts and callous disregard for Yelena's death stirred a wellspring of conflicting emotions within him, a potent brew of anger, sadness, and a dawning realization that threatened to shatter his sense of identity.

In a moment of clarity, Chel realized that he could no longer ignore the toxic legacy of his father's behavior. He could not condone the cycle of violence and indifference that had plague his family for far too long. He was not his father, and re refused to allow himself to become a reflection of the man who had brought so much pain and suffering into their lives.

"Do you have any news of Yelena's body being found?" Chel asked his father.

"Who cares?" his father shouted. "She's gone. Just another damned Demon woman, they make more every day."

"Yelena was more. Your wife is more. Do you not give a fuck about either of them?" Chel challenged the Demon. He spoke of the love and warmth that Yelena had brought into their lives, cozy evenings reading, dancing, picking flowers. The memories were a stark contrast to the darkness that his father's rage had wrought upon their family.

His father's anger boiled over, Chel stood his ground, refusing to back down. "I'm going to be better than you and if I ever have a wife or daughter I will love them more than you have ever loved anything."

"Get out of my fucking hovel with that mouth. You're nothing but a piece of shit. Hellions in my day didn't give a fuck about women or children. You were bred to serve the throne, wait, and see where this new ideology takes you all. You'll be dead in no time. And well deserved. Fuck off." Chel's father stormed off, disappearing to a room in the back of the hovel and slamming the door.

His mother hugged him. "You're a good Demon." There were tears in her eyes. "Yelena would be proud. I'm proud." She was taking off her apron and threw it aside. "I'll be leaving here now."

"I'll take you elsewhere. You can't stay here," Chel said.

She pulled a bag from under the sink. "I have only stayed this long for you, but I don't think you'll be back."

Chel shook his head. "I'll never see him again."

His mother nodded, wiping tears from her face. "There's a place I can go." She was shaking her head. "It's safe. Private."

"Good." Chel reached for the door. "Let's get you out of here."

His mother walked outside and Chel grabbed his gear and belongings. He closed the door to the hovel, taking one last glance at his family home. "Goodbye," he whispered.

Chel turned to face his mother. Walking closer, he wrapped his arm around her narrow shoulders. In that moment, Chel realized that he was not defined by the sins of his father, not bound by the chains of past Hellions. He was a warrior, a protector, and above all a son who refused to let the darkness of his father's legacy extinguish the light of hope that burned within him.

They walked down a dirt path. The sounds of furniture breaking and angry shouting came from the hovel. As they moved on, Chel vowed to honor Yelena's memory by forging a new path, one guided by empathy, tenderness, and the unwavering belief that he could be the change that his family so desperately needed.

The reign of Lucifer was over, the darkness that had infiltrated every corner of Hell was slowly dispersing.

Keep reading Midnight Serenade Now

M. R. Pritchard writes about the elemental struggle between good and evil, and gods and monsters, and about people who turn into gods and monsters. Usually with a mix of apocalypse or post-apocalyptic setting. She also includes a spec of a love story because what is humanity without love?

M. R. Pritchard is a two-time Kindle Scout winning author, her short story "Glitch" has been featured in the 2017 winter edition of THE FIRST LINE literary journal. Her short story "Moon Lord" has been featured in Chronicle Worlds: Half Way Home (Part of the Future Chronicles) and will be time capsuled on the moon on the Lunar Codex in 2024. M. R. Pritchard holds degrees in Biochemistry and Nursing. She is a northern New Yorker transplanted to the Gulf Coast of Florida who enjoys coffee, mint chocolate, cloudy days, and reading on the lanai.

Visit her website MRPritchard.com and Subscribe. You'll get subscriber only content, updates, special previews of new projects, and book deals.

<u>Steampunk:</u>

Tick of a Clockwork Heart

<u>Dark Fantasy:</u>

Sparrow Man Series/Veil of Shadows Series

Sparrow Man

Nightingale Girl

Scarecrow

Raven King

Nightjar

Night Owl

Etched in Darkness

Embrace the Night

Shadows of Destiny (forthcoming)

Midnight Serenade (forthcoming)

Thread the Bone

<u>Fantasy/Fairy Tale Love Story/Romance:</u>

Muse

Forgotten Princess Duology

Midsummer Night's Dream: A Game of Thrones

<u>Poetry/Short Stories</u>

Consequence of Gravity